MISS LIBERTY

MISS LIBERTY

ERIN MOONYEEN HALEY

STORYTIDE
An Imprint of HarperCollinsPublishers

Storytide is an imprint of HarperCollins Publishers.
Miss Liberty
Copyright © 2025 by Erin Moonyeen Haley
All rights reserved. Manufactured in Harrisonburg, VA, United States of America.
No part of this book may be used or reproduced in any manner whatsoever without written permission except in the case of brief quotations embodied in critical articles and reviews. For information, address HarperCollins Children's Books, a division of HarperCollins Publishers, 195 Broadway, New York, NY 10007.
www.harpercollinschildrens.com
Library of Congress Control Number: 2024952995
ISBN 978-0-06-336001-3
Typography by Andrea Vandergrift
25 26 27 28 29   LBC   5 4 3 2 1
First Edition

*For Moonyeen McGee,
the most glamorous "Glammy" anyone could have.*

1

It was the third Monday of June and the first day of summer vacation.

Officially Glitter Season.

Which meant that I had an excuse to pound on my sister's door at seven in the morning and yell, "Levi! Wake up. It's Glitter Season! It starts to-*day*! We got a show! Our very first one of the sum-*mer*, and I need hair help!"

"*All right*, Savvy! Knock it off!" My sister's voice was muffled, so I knew she was still in bed, probably curled like a seashell under her yellow comforter that made me feel overwhelmed and itchy with all the bees and butterflies embroidered on it. "Just get started on your makeup or something. I'll be there in a sec."

I stayed where I was, listening for movement and

checking my weather watch for the hundredth time that morning. A sun with buggy eyes and a grin beamed at me. The temperature was posted across his face. *As of right now, the temperature is—*

"Do *not* start my day with another weather report," Levi muttered.

I ignored that. "It's going to be seventy-four degrees and breezy. You were worried we'd melt while performing on asphalt, but we'll be fine."

That was the best thing about my weather watch. Its predictions gave me one less thing to worry about.

Levi muttered something I couldn't hear, so I headed to the bathroom. Nothing could upset me on this glorious Monday. It was the first day of Glitter Season and my first day as a dancer on the Liberty Line for our town, Liberté's Fourth of July parade, also known as the Miss Liberty Independence Day Parade.

People could keep their Christmas countdowns. *This* was the best time of year, a holier-than-sequins-and-red-lipstick stretch of summer—a time when actual glitter shook loose from every decoration, piling on benches, gathering in sidewalk cracks, and fairy-dusting every car from the Liberty Lady statue at Town Hall all the way to the high school.

On July Fourth, there would be a carnival during the day in the center of town with rides and games and then . . . *and then* . . . the parade!

Best day ever turns into best night ever.

And this year, I was finally in the thick of it as an *official* Liberty Line dancer! No longer in the audience, but on the stage. I would be seen, and people would compliment me like they always did with Levi and say things like I was a "natural" and was "going places."

To be a Liberty Line dancer meant that you were part of an ensemble group that's been performing in every Miss Liberty Independence Day Parade since the 1920s. Once you were in the Liberty Line—the first step to becoming Miss Liberty herself—you were basically a local celebrity.

No one was a bigger celebrity than my sister. For the past three years Levi has been Miss Liberty. On July Fourth, *she* was the main event. Not the high school marching band, not the vendors selling cotton candy swirls so big they looked like beehives on a stick, not even the guy who ran the eggbeater ride that always made at least five people puke. It was all about the parade's finale, starring Miss Liberty—her crown that sizzled gold, her sequined costume, and her Liberty Line entourage.

Hear that, universe? I'm part of Miss Liberty's entourage!

I looked at my watch again to make sure the weather hadn't suddenly changed. A blue banner appeared: *Today's weather word.* I tapped on it, and the word *troposphere* popped up along with a definition: *Refers to the lowest region of the atmosphere.*

Every time I learned a new weather word, I saved it like a penny.

A thud came from Levi's room. I figured she had stumbled against her desk while trying to pull on her tights. A dancer really shouldn't put on tights while hopping around on one leg. According to my aunt Bobbi—the queen bee of all things Miss Liberty—a dancer should always sit down, roll up the tights, and *gently* pull them on.

"I'm going to start doing my lashes!" I called.

In the bathroom, I brushed my right lash with glue, carefully aligned it with my real lash line, and pressed it down. The burning sensation was immediate; it literally felt like a wasp was stinging my eye. "Ow! Ow! Ow!"

"Oh, Savvy, stop," Levi ordered, appearing behind me in dance tights, a T-shirt, and shorts. She wouldn't put on her official costume until we got to the venue. Bobbi was adamant that important costumes like Miss Liberty's be covered up until it was time to go onstage.

"You need to put eyeliner on first and *then* align the fake lash with that. You don't just cram it on top of your regular lashes." Levi peeled the lash off and blotted the glue. "Also, we're performing at a car wash today. You don't need to worry about lashes."

"Lashes make you look better in photos, though."

I was something of an expert when it came to Miss Liberty photos. I had a shoebox full of them that I'd collected over the years. Trust me, lashes make the picture.

"Well," Levi continued, "I'm Miss Liberty, and I'm calling the shots today. No lashes."

"Fine. But that means my hair has to look *perfect*."

Today was the first of several Miss Liberty performances between now and the Fourth of July. It was going to be a car wash fundraiser to raise money for parade expenses. Even though Bobbi had never asked the dancers to participate in a fundraiser before, I loved the idea of performing more than once this summer.

"Are you sad this is your last year as Miss Liberty?" I asked. Levi had just graduated from high school, so next year the role would be up for grabs.

"Nope," Levi said, brushing my hair until it was staticky. "You know that, after this year, there will be no more parades at all, right? This is our last shebang."

"Actually," I corrected, swallowing the bit of panic in my mouth, "it's *not* the last year. Bobbi says it ain't over until it's over."

Last summer, the Town Council voted to eliminate the parade, saying it was too expensive. Bobbi, however, said that those people were shortsighted, that she'd come up with a way to keep it going.

"Because of Bobbi, I'll still get to be Miss Liberty someday," I added, wincing as Levi found a knot. "Maybe as soon as next year."

Ever since I'd made the Liberty Line, I had more confidence than I knew what to do with. It was a weird feeling.

Usually I didn't have that kind of confidence—anxiety is like a nasty overbite that can ruin every smile.

"I recommend you rethink your dreams, Savvy. Now stop fidgeting and let me work."

Levi has always been a hair genius. It helped that she was born with fantastic curls that tumbled down her back. According to Seymour, one of my best friends, who knows everything about fashion, Levi had "mermaid hair"; her curls stood out with their nutmeg and grapefruit coloring.

I have hair the color of mud, and it lies flat against my head, kind of like a helmet. But as Levi ran mousse through my scalp, I had high hopes that she'd give me volume. In the meantime, her fingers were so soft, I almost fell asleep standing up.

Until she said, "Did you hear me, Savvy? Just find a way to enjoy this year, okay?"

"There's no need. Bobbi has been brainstorming ideas to make the Town Council change its mind. That's what Tiara told me."

Tiara was my cousin and Bobbi's daughter. Even though Tiara was only six months older than me, she liked to make it seem like she was six years older, as if she were wise and sophisticated and could see things that I could not.

"Besides, I'm manifesting a buttload of confidence to make it all work out."

Levi did a snort laugh. "Is that a phrase from one of your antianxiety books?"

"They're *mindfulness* books."

Two years ago a doctor told me I "suffered" from anxiety; I hated the word *suffered* as much as I hated the word *anxiety*. Both made it sound as if I didn't have myself together, and being put together is important if you're going to be Miss Liberty. So I decided to call my anxiety Bert, and I made him my anxiety hamster. He appeared after my first audition for the Liberty Line (which I didn't make) last year, and he's made cameo appearances ever since.

In the meantime, my grandmother—better known as Glammy—has made it her business to purchase every book with a title like *Ten Tips for Your Overly Anxious Child* and *Help Your Adolescent Calm the Hurricane Within*. Dad used to do that, too, but now he and Mom are on a cross-country shopping trip so they can get their new business up and running. Since they left in the middle of May, Dad's been forwarding me articles about mental health, and Mom has been mailing me trinkets, like healing crystals from a shop in Eureka Springs, Arkansas, and a miniature Buddha from a flea market in Las Vegas.

My anxiety was basically a family affair.

"You know what I would like to manifest?" Levi began, teasing the crud out of my ponytail. "A lazy summer. Bobbi has us performing at all these extra events, and I'm hardly going to see my friends before they go off to college. Before I know it, Deja and I will be moving into our apartment in Whynot."

Seeing my stricken expression in the mirror, Levi winced. "Sorry. I know how you hate change."

She wasn't wrong. The second Levi had mentioned Whynot, my throat felt gross and mucousy, an early indicator that I was about to have a panic attack. Some people's throats get dry; mine always felt like it was full of phlegm that was going to make me puke.

I tried to focus on things I was looking forward to. "I think all the performances will be fun. We have today for the car wash, then performances at Shuckey's, and the Honeybee Fair—"

"You're forgetting how she made *me* go to Tires and Treads two weeks ago for their big sale. Man, that was boring."

"Well, when I'm Miss Liberty, I'm gonna walk around in my costume all day, every day, doing whatever Bobbi wants and posing for a million pictures. And you know why?"

"Why?"

"Because being Miss Liberty is the secret to getting everything you want in life. The second that crown is on your head, all sorts of doors open. Everybody sees you, and everybody loves you."

"If you say so." Levi yawned.

I couldn't believe she didn't see it; there were so many examples. The anchor on *Talk Now*? Former Miss Liberty. The model for the new Surf & Shorts campaign? Former Miss Liberty. Those three Rockettes who always get the most camera time during the Macy's Thanksgiving Day Parade? All former Miss Libertys. My aunt Bobbi, Dad's sister, who now runs the dance studio and all things Miss Liberty? Former Miss Liberty.

Then, of course, my personal favorite, Yvette Rayne, Miss Liberty turned meteorologist for Channel 4, who constantly used magnificent weather words like *vorticity*, *adiabatic*, *macroburst*, *dew-point depression*, and, my favorite, *pineapple express*. That's a condition where wet and warm air flows up from the tropics ahead of a massive winter storm, dumping rain and snow in the Pacific Northwest.

Each of those women were first *seen* because of the parade, and no one has overlooked them since.

That's who I was going to be—the girl no one overlooked.

2

After Levi finished my hair, I followed her to her room while she finished getting ready.

I loved hanging out in my sister's room, with its fairy lights and dance posters of Bob Fosse, Maria Tallchief, and Misty Copeland. Not to mention that it had been a while since my sister and I had gotten ready for the same event. It was like we were finally existing in the same galaxy at the same time!

"It would be nice if Mom and Dad were here," Levi said, applying thick eyeliner that reminded me of an old Cleopatra movie we watched with Glammy.

I tried not to think about my parents, on account of missing them too much. They'd both quit their jobs in March to launch their own business. Currently, they were driving around America trying to find "kitschy and funky" items for their "kitschy and funky" store. They called when they could, and we Zoomed, but Glammy said they really needed to focus on making this store a success. In the beginning, they called once a week. Now it was once in a blue moon.

"Alrighty, let me see how beautiful we all are," Glammy sang, popping her head in. "Holy hairspray and hairdos, you girls look amazing!" And she added, "Savvy, before you go, put your tapping stage back under the bed. I need to vacuum later."

My tapping stage was five planks of wood that Dad had hammered together so I could practice tap dancing anytime I wanted without scuffing up the kitchen floor.

Tapping was my favorite thing in the world, except for Miss Liberty. It wasn't just the physical act of tapping that I loved; it was the sounds, especially when no music was playing and I could hear my own feet. Tap was the only time I felt like I actually knew what I was doing, both in life and on the stage. When I tapped, my body felt strong, and I could move it the way I wanted. I could move as fast as I needed to move. I could be heavy and loud and get lost in the moment with every scuff and shuffle as I grinded up my worries like coffee beans.

"Now," Glammy continued, "no tears if the turnout for today is disappointing. Remember those ladies at the grocery store, Sav?"

Glammy and I had been waiting at the checkout when the two women in front of us—super noticeable because they were both wearing tennis outfits the color of highlighters—started talking about the parade.

"I'm just going to say it," said Orange Highlighter. "I wish we weren't going to be here for the Fourth. Last year's parade was depressing. But I waited too long to check out rentals, and now every place at the Shore is all booked up."

Glammy had given me a look that meant *Be quiet, Savvy. Not your beans, not your business.*

"The fireworks were pathetic," Pink Highlighter had agreed.

Pathetic? I could *not* believe she had used that word.

"I'll try to make it today, but no guarantees," Glammy added. "I've got a shift at Nifty Thrifty." She kissed me and then Levi on the forehead. "Savvy, we really could use an extra pair of hands to wade through donations, and now that it's summer—"

"Sorry, Glammy, I'm one hundred percent focused on making this the best parade ever," I replied.

Glammy gave a dramatic sigh. "*Fine.* Never hurts to ask. Don't forget movie night tonight. I'll see you divas later." She blew us each a kiss and was gone with as much energy as she came in with.

Levi got up and dug through her closet. I knew she was going to bring out the Miss Liberty costume in five, four, three . . .

"Sav. Get your stuff and listen for Deja's car. We don't need much. Just a water bottle."

"And my tap shoes."

"Savvy, you don't need to take your tap shoes *everywhere*."

"Yes I do! What if something happens and Bobbi needs me to distract the audience with a solo? What if a choreographer shows up looking for fresh talent? What if—"

"Your 'what if's' are making *me* anxious. Just go," Levi said, shoving me out into the hall. "I'll meet you downstairs."

With that, she shut the door in my face, and I was right back where I started this morning.

3

We heard Deja pull into the driveway before she even beeped her horn. I didn't know much about cars, but I was pretty sure her Mazda wasn't supposed to sound like a garbage disposal. It was also covered in bumper stickers, most of which asked really personal questions like, *Have you balanced your chakras today?* and *Are you victimizing the planet with fast fashion?*

Deja used to dance, and I still couldn't believe that she gave it up to compete in swimming. Because of the swim team, she kept her hair cut in an angled bob that she could cram under her swim cap. I remember when her hair was long and glorious, like a blue-black waterfall.

"Let's go, Liberty Ladies!" Deja shouted.

"Coming!" I called, stepping onto the porch.

Levi was right behind me. In one hand she carried *the* Miss Liberty costume, carefully protected by an old bag from the dry cleaner's. The plastic did nothing to hide its sparkles; I could clearly see the cheerleader-style skirt pleated with red, white, and blue panels. The white corset was bedazzling on its own, with red, white, blue, gold, silver, and bronze sequins. It was so special that Bobbi had to borrow a tent from the local greenhouse so Levi could change out of her regular clothes and into her costume after she arrived at the car wash. Bobbi was serious about keeping costumes immaculate.

"What's that?" I asked, noticing one of dad's accordion folders poking out of her gym bag.

"Just some . . . college financial stuff I need to send in," Levi said. "Let's go." She skipped ahead of me, fizzy with energy she hadn't had an hour earlier.

I climbed into the back seat, and Levi sat shotgun. For a moment I felt like I was seventeen instead of twelve. Hanging out with my sister and her friends had that effect.

"Ah, the sacred costume has been brought forth, ready for its last summer in the sun," Deja proclaimed.

"Don't tease," Levi chided, nodding in my direction. "There's a diehard in our midst."

I didn't respond. I was too busy pulling my shorts down a bit so that Deja's seats wouldn't scald my thighs.

My costume wasn't anything special: blue shorts and white T-shirt. But for our performances at the Honeybee

Fair and the actual parade, I would be wearing a red, white, and blue costume that was similar to Miss Liberty's. Not as fancy, but close, and close was good enough for me.

Deja turned onto Constitution Avenue and stopped at a red light that was directly in front of *her*: the glorious statue of Liberty Lady, who rose like a mythical figure from a stone platform in front of Town Hall.

"As long as *she's* here, the parade won't disappear," I whispered, clasping my hands in prayer because, heck, why not?

The Miss Liberty legend was of epic importance to our town, even though no one was a hundred percent sure whether it was real or not. During the Revolutionary War, the British seized our town and used it to store gunpowder. Supposedly, the Liberty Lady—a colonial woman whose real name has been lost to history—got a bunch of her friends to sneak into the storage area and get rid of the gunpowder by lighting it up. British soldiers abandoned the town that very night because the explosions gave the illusion of a massive attack. Word spread that the Liberty Lady and her friends had tricked the enemy, and that's how the Miss Liberty title was born.

Our town was called Liberté because, around that same time, a bunch of French soldiers who were garrisoned here heard the legend and slapped the name on the village. Still, no one pronounced it with a French accent. Anyone who did was obviously from out of town.

The light turned green.

"When people see us on the Fourth, they'll remember how important the parade and Miss Liberty are to our town, and they won't let it go anywhere," I declared.

"Don't hold your breath," my sister hummed, which was not the vibe anyone wanted from their Miss Liberty.

4

The second we hopped out of the car, Deja roared away, yelling, "Have fun!"

Levi stared after her longingly. "She's going to be partying at the Shore all weekend."

I traced my finger along the sequins of her Miss Liberty costume that were puckering through the plastic. "Being here is better," I insisted.

Levi looked down at me. I was surprised when she smiled. "You're right. And today, everyone will see Miss Liberty in a whole new light."

I stopped tracing the costume. "What does that mean?"

"Gotta go change." And she ran into the tent, which took up at least four parking spaces.

"Savvy Montrose, you're *not* wearing your lashes."

Whipping around, I came face-to-face with Tiara, who was wearing lashes as thick as curtain fringe.

Without asking, she reached out and began to pull on my eyelid. "You didn't even put on the individual lashes. Not that you could. Those take patience *and* skill."

"Levi said we didn't have to wear lashes today. She said—"

"*Ew*. Make sure you wash your hands after touching Savvy's eyes," Mina said, an elbow on Tiara's shoulder. She was one of Tiara's best friends. Her mom—Dottie—was our seamstress, who also worshiped at the altar of all things Miss Liberty. "Eyes are notorious for having germs."

"Oh, get real, Mina," Stevie, another of Tiara's best friends, chided. She crossed her arms over her chest.

"My eyes do not have germs," I snapped.

I don't know if all dance studios had a hierarchy of bossiness, but ours sure did. It went like this: If my aunt wasn't there to boss us all around, then Dottie was, but since Dottie was usually glued to Bobbi's side, that left Tiara to do the bossing. And if Tiara wasn't there to order everyone around, then Stevie or Mina were.

Tiara took a step back, studying me. "Well, you're in the back line for part of the dance. I guess no one will notice. Now, come on, everyone is lining up. Bobbi is especially tense today."

As we got into position, I couldn't help but think how lucky Tiara was—she got to call her mom by her first name. I tried that once with my mom, and it just got me grounded for the weekend.

"This is so exciting," Seymour said, wrapping his arms around my waist. He was one of my best friends and the only guy we had in our Liberty Line. "We're finally in the number together!"

"Let's make it perfect," I whispered, scanning the parking lot. There were two cars parked and two cars waiting to be washed after we performed. Hardly any people were watching, mostly parents.

"Where is everyone?" I muttered.

"It's only our first show of the summer," he said. "Don't worry. Besides, look! There's Dulce. I bet she'll post an article and get people excited. She's got twenty-five followers."

Seymour possessed an amazing kind of optimism that never became dented or scratched, no matter what came up in life. It would be an annoying trait on anyone else, but on him, it fit.

I just thought, *Twenty-five doesn't sound like that much. We need more than that supporting us.*

Dulce was standing next to Mrs. Bardot, Seymour's mom. Dulce caught my eye, waved, and went back to readying her pen over her clipboard. A couple of times a week she posted an article on her website, *History Fits*, an online newsletter that's a play on the phrase *hissy fits*. She wrote about the bits and pieces of history that were overlooked.

She said it annoyed her when people only studied the big battles and royalty, so she published *History Fits* instead of throwing a real hissy fit.

The music began. We slapped on big smiles, held the first thirty-six counts, then did jazz runs out onto the staging area, which was set up so close to the car wash that there were little puddles we had to avoid. We performed our sequence, eventually scooting forward to meet the other groups for a kickline, and we dropped to our knees and held out our right hands in a *ta-dah* gesture.

Levi appeared next in her Miss Liberty costume. She sparkled like a Windexed chandelier, the silvers, reds, and blues catching the afternoon light. As fantastic as the costume was, it was the crown that *really* showed her off, clamped to her head with at least fifty bobby pins.

The Miss Liberty crown was no joke. It was an architectural wonder, a lacework pyramid of red, blue, and crystal rhinestones arranged in a fading fashion that Bobbi calls *ombré*. It was a crown that meant business. Sparkly business.

"Whoo-ooo, Miss Liberty!" Mrs. Bardot shouted, clapping and whistling.

Levi took a few supermodel steps (Seymour's term, not mine) to back up. Then she launched into her turns—*epic* turns, where she spun so fast it was like the balls of her feet were covered in creamy peanut butter.

We Liberty Line dancers held our poses.

After spinning until she was a blur, Levi bowed, and we

hustled to join her in a straight line. That's when we rippled in a series of hinge kicks, dropped down, shot back up, and nailed a final pose.

It was glorious. I waited for the roar of applause to wash over me, but it didn't come. Instead I heard a confetti toss of clapping.

Levi blew kisses in every direction as Bobbi joined her center stage. Bobbi was thematically dressed in a blouse with a flag embroidered on the back and khakis covered in blue and red rhinestones as big as beetles.

"Thank you, thank you, thank you, residents of Liberté!" Bobbi gushed. "And let's hear it for Levi Montrose, my niece, our Miss Liberty for the *third year in a row*."

People clapped as Bobbi reintroduced Levi and the rest of the Liberty Line. Bobbi also talked about our upcoming Honeybee Fair performance and the parade. She didn't say a word about this being the parade's final year, which I took as a positive sign.

While she was talking, Levi stepped away to pull her gym bag out from under a chair.

Bobbi barely noticed. "You know how we love to entertain you, and this fundraiser is one of several performances we're doing to ramp up excitement for Liberté's favorite holiday: Fourth of July! No one celebrates our nation's birthday like we do, am I right? But right now I'd like to take a minute to give Dottie some love. I know that these girls—and Seymour—look like they're wearing just white

T-shirts and shorts, but it does take work to make them all look so polished."

Dottie trotted out, clapping and giggling, wearing a shirt very similar to Bobbi's. She and Bobbi exchanged cheek kisses before Bobbi faced front again.

I, however, was watching my sister, who had pulled out Dad's accordion folder and was removing a stack of papers.

"So, once again, our next event will be in front of Shuckey's Arcade tomorrow night, Tuesday, and I know Mayor Radnor and I can count on you all to be there."

Bobbi gestured toward the mayor. He was impossible to miss, being so tall and lanky. He reminded me of a vintage Gumby toy that Mom and Dad bought in Amarillo, Texas.

"Bobbi!" Levi called. "If you don't mind, I'd like to say something."

"Oh?" It took Bobbi a beat to hide her surprise. "Well . . . um . . . of course, Miss Liberty, by all means."

Instead of returning to center stage, my sister walked past Bobbi to weave her way through the minuscule crowd, passing out papers as if she were handing out a test.

"Since this is my final year as Miss Liberty, I've been doing a lot of thinking—" Levi began. "In my honors civics class this past semester, we talked a lot about the idea of liberty, and how it has to be guarded and nurtured every day. It occurred to me that while Miss Liberty is in a perfect position to guard and nurture, she never does. She just smiles and stays mute, like a figurine on a shelf. That made me realize I've been missing opportunities to educate people in this community about areas where liberty is being trampled."

I glanced at Bobbi. She was gripping her pearls so tightly I could see them biting into the back of her neck.

"No doubt Miss Liberty is a symbol," Levi continued, "but people seem to think she's *just* a symbol, that as long as she's in this costume, she doesn't need to do or be anything else. I disagree. If a person is called Miss Liberty, shouldn't that person be proactive? Shouldn't she point out areas where liberty is faltering and then rally the citizens to do something? So that's what I'm going to be doing this summer. I'm going to be acting as I think Miss Liberty would if she were a living, breathing human instead of some caricature or cartoon."

My throat was dry. *Is my sister concussed?* Miss Liberty was *never* a cartoon. She was an *icon*.

"And what I want to talk about is voting."

"Voting?" Bobbi asked, finding her voice but keeping her "all is well" smile in place. "Levi, we're here to have fun and raise money to keep the parade afloat—"

"I'm almost done, Bobbi, I promise," Levi interrupted. "The flyers I've been handing out are about a protest I'm organizing. In case you all missed it, our voting center closed a few weeks ago and is going to be reopened forty miles *outside of town*. It will also be the voting location for *three* other towns, including the much larger town of

Whynot. That's ridiculous! Some of us are going to have a hard enough time making it to the new location, but what if the wait time to vote is one or two or three *hours*? What if the wait time is *all day*? That means some people might not vote; their voices won't be heard. As this town's longest-running Miss Liberty, I'm going to stage a protest at the courthouse on July fifth."

"Um, Miss Liberty . . . Levi, *dear*," Bobbi said. "All these good people are going to be attending my Liberty Luncheon at that time, *remember*?" Bobbi turned toward Dottie, who handed her a clipboard. Bobbi held up the clipboard and continued. "You see these blank pieces of paper? They're blank *petition* pages. Once I have the signature of every citizen, it will be clear that we all love the parade too much to let it go. The Town Council will have to recommit funds to make it continue."

Levi pressed her lips together. "With all due respect, Bobbi, the voting issue is more important than the parade."

Dead silence. Everyone—and I mean *everyone*—was looking between my aunt and Levi.

It was Levi who broke the awkward silence. "And besides, Bobbi, I'm sure that people can attend both." She curtsied, blew a kiss, and strutted back into her tent.

No one moved, except for Seymour, who leaned toward me, whispering, "I don't know what's going on, but it all feels fierce. Very fierce."

5

For the past eight minutes and forty-eight seconds—the time it took for my weather watch to inform me that the temperature had dropped one degree—Levi and Bobbi had been huddled in the tent.

My sister had broken a rule. A *sacred* rule. Not one that was written down, but one that existed nonetheless. Since the dawn of time, Miss Liberty posed, danced, and wore the world's biggest crown. She kissed babies on cheeks and waved at young dancers who wanted to be her one day. She kept her lips glossy and her eyelashes straight. She was photogenic and glamorous.

She rarely spoke. She *never* spoke about issues. And she never, *ever* protested.

I heard Dottie yell for dry towels. Some of the youngest

girls were washing a truck, but it was clear this fundraiser was a dud. There were buckets full of soap that hadn't been touched.

"I don't hear yelling," Seymour said, pressing his ear gently to the tent. He, Tiara, Mina, Stevie, and I were all straining to hear. It wasn't long before Dulce joined us.

"I took some great photos to go with my article," she whispered to me.

That's when I saw that she had an iPhone in her hands. "You got a phone?" I swear, everyone had a phone but me.

"My mom got some two-for-one deal. You know she can't resist those."

Dulce's mom shopped like it was an Olympic sport. It was a compulsion that was gossiped about all over town. Dulce tried to pretend it didn't bother her.

"I have a new idea," Dulce continued. "I'm thinking of writing a full history of the parade for my website, something to draw in more traffic, which is why I'm going to be writing *and* taking photos. I'm thinking of calling it '*The Legacy of Miss Liberty: A Parade History*.'"

"Legacy?" Mina demanded. "Our Miss Liberty just got political, so I think she tanked her legacy. And where are the reporters? I thought Channel 4 was coming today."

"Yvette Rayne couldn't be here. She's at the Shore. There's a storm rolling in and she gets to cover it."

"She's just a weatherperson," Mina snipped. "I meant a *real* reporter."

I was about to snap that Yvette Rayne *was* a real reporter, when my head started to pound. I had been trying to submerge my uneasy emotions, and now they were rising up from my belly all at once, like lava.

"Would you really have wanted a reporter here to see Levi's meltdown?" Tiara asked me sourly.

I pressed my palms to my cheeks. "She didn't have a meltdown." *Why oh why am I defending my sister?*

"Hey, Savvy, you okay?" Seymour whispered. "You look flushed."

I shook my head.

"Oh wait, this will help." He pulled out a red, white, and blue feather fan from his bag, tickling my nose as he waved it in front of my face. Seymour had an extensive collection of fans: fans that were painted and fans that were glittered. All of them looked like they belonged on the stage or in the movies.

"Bobbi is going to be freaking out for the rest of the week." Tiara groaned.

"What's the big deal?" Stevie asked. "Levi wants a closer voting location. It makes sense."

"Oh my gosh, Stevie, are you serious?" Mina asked. "Miss Liberty is supposed to just stand there and look pretty. That's what my mom says, anyway."

"Sounds outdated," Dulce muttered.

Bobbi flung back the tent flaps and stormed past us, Levi right behind her.

"Bobbi," my sister was saying, "just listen . . ."

Seymour looked at me, still waving his fan. "Is this working?"

I shook my head and stared at the ground. Whenever I'm fighting a panic attack, I try not to talk. *Focus on your breathing.*

I envisioned my chest expanding like it was filled with warm zephyrs (a Yvette weather word meaning soft, gentle breezes). Yvette says that warm winds move more slowly than cold air, and I wanted everything inside of me to slow down.

"Hey, Levi!" I heard someone call. It was Mrs. DiBrillo, who wrote articles for our local paper, the *Herald*. "When you can spare a second, I'd love to get a few photos."

Levi flashed her toothpaste smile. "Oh, of course! Why don't I hold up my flyer while you take the picture?"

"That's okay. I'd rather just have you in your costume."

"Hi, Levi!" Mrs. Dickson called from the other direction. "I gotta ask, how do you keep your hair in that perfect ponytail? I just can't tame Gracie's flyaways."

Levi twirled the tip of her ponytail, which meant she was thinking. We were hair twirlers in my family. "Hairspray, I guess. And gel . . . gel is the key to everything."

"Any products you recommend?"

"Um." Levi's jaw clenched. I could tell she was annoyed. "Lush and Lovely is pretty good. Hey, Mrs. Dickson, your husband manages the electronic store over in Belford, doesn't he? Do you think he could help me get a microphone and sound system? You know, for the protest?"

Mrs. Dickson glanced in Bobbi's direction, but Bobbi was talking to the mayor.

"Um, sure. I can ask," she said.

Just as Mrs. Dickson was about to take a picture, Levi grabbed a flyer and snuck it into the shot.

I closed my eyes. It felt as if someone was pressing their thumbs against my temples, gripping my head like it was a football.

I knew my panic attack was going to hit a new level of intensity a half second before it did. The nausea peaked, and my body went cold from the inside out, like an iceberg was melting in my belly. As the cold spread, my eyeballs started to feel tight.

Suddenly I couldn't breathe. Bright asterisks starred my eyesight. I bent down, putting my hands on my knees, trying to stabilize myself.

Later, I would learn that Seymour had shouted for Levi to come over. At the time, it felt like my sister magically appeared, placing one hand flat against my sternum and the other flat against my back, as if I were a doll she was keeping upright. She did that whenever anxiety choked my breathing.

"Is she having an asthma attack?" I heard Mina ask.

"She's having a panic attack," Levi said. "It happens from time to time."

This is so embarrassing. Bert, knock it off.

When everything in my body finally decided to slow down, I had no idea how much time had passed.

"You okay, Savvy?" Dulce asked.

"She'll be fine," Levi said, using her most adult voice.

"I'm okay," I said, straightening up. Now that I had my voice again, I was able to glare at Levi. "You lied to me. You said those papers were for college. You didn't say anything about using Miss Liberty to make everyone think of boring and depressing things like voting."

"Voting is not boring," Levi said. "Things are happening that worry me."

"Since when?"

"Since I realized that I don't want to dance and pose every day for the rest of my life. Since I found something *meaningful* to care about."

"Miss Liberty *is* meaningful! She's important and special as is." What I didn't say was that Miss Liberty made me believe I was going to hit all my goals, because that's what *all* Miss Libertys do!

"No, Savvy. Miss Liberty is meaningful if you care only about appearances." Levi straightened up. "This is my last year, and I'm not going out in a way that's silly and frivolous. And if this costume is going to silence me, I guess I need a new outfit." With that, she walked away.

I couldn't believe her. She didn't care that I *needed* Miss Liberty. She didn't care that without that title and crown, I had nothing to look forward to.

6

"Walk with me, Savvy."

At the sound of Bobbi's voice, I jumped a mile. It was a quarter after seven and everyone was cleaning up. Except for Levi. Another of her school friends had picked her up around four, so she had escaped wringing out the rags and stacking the buckets.

"Really? Me? Okay . . . great. Sure."

Even though Bobbi and I were on the same wavelength about many things, we rarely had one-on-one conversations. I was feeling excited and nervous as we walked over to her car. She lifted up the hatch, giving us a place to sit. "I want you to know that I'm doing everything in my power to keep the parade here."

"I believe you. And I think you can do it. If anyone can, it's you."

Bobbi looked at me like I was her new best friend. "Thank you for saying that. I was expecting Levi to help me out, but she seems to have her own agenda. She forgets the power of Miss Liberty—that once people see the costume, they remember all the parades they've seen and how they're part of this town's lineage and their family histories. That's why the dances have stayed the same; people love tradition. It's comforting. Oh, I suppose I could institute *some* changes. Instead of you all kicking in a line and then a circle, we could do an inverted V or—"

When she paused to think, I realized this could be my moment.

"Or," I began, clicking the heels of my sneakers together, "if you want to add something, but not a big something, I could do a tap solo. I practice all the time."

Bobbi took her hand off her pearls to fluff my ponytail.

"Such a sweet suggestion. Maybe we can arrange for you to have a solo in the recital next year. Now, I could use your help on another matter. Let me know if this 'protest' Levi has planned gets any traction. I'm sure it won't, but I'd like to be kept in the loop. I've got to be on top of things."

"I can help you be on top of things."

"Fan-tastic!" She clapped her hands together. "If you think about it, it's all so silly, what Levi is grumbling about. She acts like we're being denied the right to vote. We just have to drive a little farther. Hardly worth complaining about. I believe that the more Levi performs in costume, the more she'll remember how important it is to have Miss

Liberty as a symbol of American pride. After all, there's never been a protesting Miss Liberty. Why start now?"

"Right." I nodded. I remembered my dad once complaining that his sister was too intense, but that was silly. She was passionate and determined, I totally got that.

"I'm glad you and I are on the same page. And try to watch those panic attacks, okay? They don't do anyone any good." My aunt patted my hand, hopped off the car, and walked away.

I wanted to remind her that I didn't have panic attacks on purpose, but I decided against it. She had enough on her plate.

My weather watch beeped, telling me that it was an hour until sunset. Looking in the direction of the Liberty Lady statue, I saw a sky that was the color of melting Skittles in a sweaty palm, all purples and oranges swirling together. I wondered if there was a name for that kind of sunset. While I was pretty sure that there wasn't, I wondered if I could make up my own sky terms one day and use my Miss Liberty fame to help them catch on.

7

A little after eight-thirty, when everything was finally cleaned up, Dulce, Seymour, and I told Mrs. Bardot we were walking home. It was too nice of a night to be in a car.

Just as we started down Amendment Way, Tiara and Stevie jogged up to join us.

"We're walking with you guys," Tiara announced. "I *need* a Bobbi break."

"O-*kay*," Seymour said, giving me a questioning look. Tiara & Co. rarely wanted to be with us.

"Where's Mina?" I asked.

"Helping her mom take stuff back to the studio," Stevie replied.

Dulce paused, taking a picture of the Amendment Way

street sign. When she saw my confused look, she said, "If I'm going to do a historical reflection of the parade, I need establishing shots of the town."

"Historical reflection?" Stevie asked.

"Yep. Instead of writing individual articles about different historical facts, I'm going to do a series of articles, including pictures of the parade."

"And *I'm* going to help with the pictures," I said.

"Sounds like you two just gave yourself homework for the summer," Stevie pointed out.

"So, Savvy," Tiara began, sliding between me and Seymour. "What were you and Bobbi talking about over by the car?"

I could hear twinges of jealousy in Tiara's voice. It was super rare that she was jealous of me. She was always the first to know everything and to do everything. She took swim lessons before me, she took dance lessons before me, she had her ears pierced before me, and she got a phone before me.

"*We* were talking about Levi and how *I* need to let your mom know if any of the protest talk is real," I said. "Bobbi trusts me."

"It's not trust, Savvy," Tiara countered. "You live with Levi. You're the one who can spy on her the easiest."

"Let's face it, guys," Stevie said, walking along the curb like it was a balance beam. "The parade has gotten a little sad. There were hardly any fireworks last year."

"Good thing *she's* not around to see this sad day," Seymour said solemnly. He had stopped walking and was pointing to the Liberty Lady statue.

For a moment, no one said anything.

"As the local historian, you know what I think?" Dulce softly said. "You all need to drum up a bit of nostalgia. Best way to get everyone psyched up."

I tilted my head to study the statue. "Like memories?"

Dulce nodded. "Yeah, but memories with a *feeling*. Like how my dad gets when he listens to his old Nirvana CD. Or, like how Mom felt last week when she outbid some other shopper on something called Jordache jeans."

"Jordache jeans?" Stevie asked.

"Jeans that were popular in the eighties," Seymour said.

Dulce took a photo of the statue. "I don't really get it. But yeah, those things gave Mom the warm fuzzies of nostalgia. People in town don't have the warm fuzzies about the parade anymore." She shoved her phone in her back pocket. "Listen, I gotta put this article together. See you guys later."

"I'll walk with you," Seymour called to her. "I left my iPad at your house." He looked at me. "You good?"

I nodded. "Yep. Bye."

While Dulce and Seymour headed off, Tiara, Stevie, and I stayed where we were.

"Nostalgia," Stevie said slowly. "How do we do that?"

No one had an answer; we all just stood there thinking.

As the silence stretched, I started to tap a sequence of steps to wake up my brain.

"Everyone has family photos of the parade," I pointed out. "And I bet just looking at them gives them warm fuzzies."

Tiara smacked her hands together. "That's it! All we need to do is hang a bunch of pictures to get people thinking about how much they love the parade. Let's all go home and get every photo from every Miss Liberty event that we can find."

"What if our photos are on our parents' phones?" Stevie asked.

Tiara rolled her eyes. "Email them to me, and I'll print them." She glanced around and dropped her voice to a whisper. "Let's meet back here at midnight. I'll call Mina."

"Why?" I asked. This was moving a bit fast for me. "What are we going to be doing?"

"Putting the photos up, silly."

"Midnight?" Stevie hissed. "I'm not allowed to go anywhere at midnight."

"So sneak out."

"No way. We have a house alarm."

Tiara shook her hands like she was drying her nails. "Guys, we have to do this when it's dark. Savvy, can't you sneak out? Your parents have basically abandoned you."

"They haven't abandoned me!"

"It's a yes or no question."

I thought about it. "Yes, I can sneak out."

"Stevie, you can sleep over at my house tonight. Mina too. We'll sneak out through the basement. Savvy, you'll meet us here. Midnight. And everyone bring Scotch tape and pictures. This is a total Bobbi move. We should be proud of ourselves."

8

When I got home, Glammy met me at the door with two DVDs. Without looking, I knew they were musicals.

"Sorry I didn't make it to the show," she said. "Nifty Thrifty was overwhelmed with donations. *But*, since today was your first performance, I'll let you pick tonight's movie: *Morocco* with Marlene Dietrich or *The Wizard of Oz* with Judy Garland."

"*Morocco*. I've seen *The Wizard of Oz*."

"Perfect. Let's get out the ice cream." She paused and tilted her head. "You okay? You look tired."

"I think I'm just a little sunburned."

She reached out and stroked my chin, tickling me with her orange-red acrylic nails. "Well, wash up. I made the spiciest jerk chicken imaginable. We're going to be sweating while we watch our movie."

Ever since Glammy moved in, movie nights had become a regular thing. For starters, we only watched DVDs; we never streamed. Glammy liked to read the back of the DVD case while the movie was playing.

We all had our spots in the living room: Levi on Dad's wingback chair (the color of pickles) and Glammy and I under a blanket on a couch that was so old, it sank in the middle, creating a crater between the cushions. Levi always got out the paper napkins and utensils, and I always put out the TV trays.

"Sorry for bolting out of there, Savvy," Levi said, bounding down the stairs. "But I figured you'd walk home. Funny how we can walk everywhere in this town except to our voting station."

"Whatever." I didn't have the energy to think about my sister. Glancing at my watch, I saw that it was 9:02. In two hours, fifty-eight minutes and zero seconds I had to sneak out and meet Tiara and somehow make this whole "nostalgia" thing work for us. Unlike Stevie, sneaking out wouldn't be a problem for me. Levi and Glammy were heavy sleepers, especially Glammy. Nothing can wake her up except a tornado siren or the smell of burning bacon.

"Let's settle in for movie night," Glammy announced, waitressing in our plates.

"You know you're going to fall asleep halfway through, Glammy," Levi teased.

"I will not," Glammy protested.

Levi and I just giggled, because we knew better.

"So, I'm going to assume the first event of the season was a blast?" Glammy asked as the DVD tray opened and shut a few times in a row.

"It was kinda sad," Levi said. "There was hardly anyone there."

"I didn't think you noticed," I grumbled, sinking deeper into the couch. "You were so focused on your protest talk."

Glammy turned her head. To my surprise, she *smiled* at Levi. "So you went through with it? You handed out the flyers?"

I looked from Glammy to Levi and back again. "Glammy, you knew about this?"

"Of course. Your sister knows I attended protests back in the day. I was quite the political agitator. Levi asked me for advice. I said that her instincts to hold a demonstration the day after the Fourth of July parade were spot-on."

"Thank you," Levi sang in an annoying trill.

"Well, *I* talked to Bobbi, and this is the worst timing," I retorted. "She and I believe—"

"Let's not talk about the parade and the protests," Glammy interrupted. "I'm proud of both of you for having such strong convictions, and I know your parents are too."

"Don't mention them," I said. "They ditched us."

Glammy clucked her tongue. "Holy hairspray and hairdos, they did not ditch you. They're doing what is best for the family. You should be proud to have parents who aren't afraid to take risks."

"I know *I* am," Levi said.

Glammy eased back on the couch and patted my knee. "Let's just bask in the brilliance of Marlene Dietrich. Fun fact: because of this movie, I wore a tux during my talent competition for Miss College Sweetheart."

"Really?" Levi asked, picking up the remote. "I think we need to see a photo for proof." Then she smiled and winked at me, like we hadn't *just* been fighting.

"Oh, Levi, don't skip this part," Glammy called out, pointing at the screen.

"It's a trailer, Glam."

"No, it's a *compilation* of Dietrich's greatest hits. I love when they put these in front of movies. Reminds me of what I need to rewatch."

Levi let the greatest hits play. As we watched the career of Dietrich play out in excerpts and snippets, I kept looking between my grandma and my sister, wondering how I was even related to the women in my family. How could I possibly be from the same gene pool as people who got over fights easily and who seemed confident all the time? How could I be related to women who always got what they wanted the *first* time around?

Case in point #1: Glammy has been a beauty pageant winner in over thirty-two small competitions. Miss Avocado, Miss Gas n' Go, Miss Seashell . . . and on and on.

Case in point #2: Mom became a California Girl after her first tryout. The California Girls were a dance group in Southern California that performed for the NBA team San Diego Sunshine. After that, she did tons of modeling. Her breakthrough job had been for Levi's jeans, hence my sister's name.

Case in point #3: Levi, Miss Liberty herself. Miss Perfect.

Then there's me, orbiting Planet Perfect.

I guess by now I should be used to the fact that all the women in my family are composed of stardust and diamonds. I'm made from cubic zirconia, like the earrings we have to wear when performing, the ones that look like diamonds but aren't, so it's okay if they get lost. They're just the fake stuff, anyway.

All through the movie, I kept my eye on the clock.

The plot was easy to follow. Marlene played a singer named Amy Jolly who was a cabaret performer in Morocco. The best scene was in the beginning, when Dietrich strutted onto the smoky floor of a nightclub wearing a tuxedo.

"Wow," Levi breathed.

"She looks amazing, doesn't she?" Glammy asked.

Levi nodded. "Look at all the other women in their fancy dresses. She's showing them who's boss in that tux."

"Why is she boss for wearing a tux?" I asked.

"Isn't it obvious?" Levi chided through a mouthful of popcorn. "She's *supposed* to look a certain way: feminine and soft and pretty. In the tux, she's saying that she doesn't care about pretty. She's being fearless. Being fearless makes her boss."

Before the movie ended, Glammy fell asleep on the couch. A little later, Levi yawned, stretched, and announced she was heading upstairs to take a shower.

It was ten thirty and seventy-four degrees when the movie ended. Glammy was still snoring, and I could hear Levi in the bathroom doing her epically long skin-care routine. To kill time, I headed to my room and pulled out my mini stage.

"Maybe this will help you sleep. Tire you out," Mom had said when Dad gave it to me.

But it hadn't.

Not that it was the stage's fault. To be honest, I'm hardly ever tired, which is why I've always dreaded bedtime. Of course, that dread makes my anxiety worse, and then I become obsessed over bedtime, and the anxiety builds, and not even Bert can cope with the hurricane of worry.

To avoid making too much noise, I tapped in my

sneakers. The whole time, I thought about Marlene Dietrich's greatest hits. I wondered what my greatest hits reel would look like. Probably pretty boring. A few dance photos and some snippets from the annual recital.

Taking a break from tapping, I went downstairs, took Glammy's phone from her charger in the kitchen and logged onto *History Fits*. Dulce had already posted her latest article, pictures included. I immediately saw a photo of my sister and Bobbi, Levi on one side of the audience and Bobbi on the other. I don't remember that they had been standing *that* far apart, but I guess they were.

As Glammy would say, Holy hairspray and hairdos. This better not be a bad omen for the rest of the summer.

VOTING: WHAT'S IT ALL ABOUT?

FROM THE DESK OF DULCE MARIE MONTOYA

Voting. Where does one begin? Our Miss Liberty made a heartfelt speech at today's car wash fundraiser. She wanted everyone to pay attention to the fact that our voting location has been moved to the outside of town. While Miss Liberty's proactivity certainly got tongues wagging (not everyone thinks that Miss Liberty should have an opinion), it also got this reporter and historian thinking. What should a town like ours—one that loves its Fourth of July parade— know about the history of voting? According to

the Library of Congress, the first time voters got to choose between candidates who came from competing political parties was in 1796. That got me thinking: Is competition at the root of voting, and therefore at the root of democracy?
Is cooperation less important?

9

When I left the house, a waxing gibbous moon was rising. Those moons are easy to spot because they look like lumpy, luminescent turtle shells. The air felt sticky and heavy; according to my weather watch, the humidity had spiked to sixty-four. There was a red flag next to that number. When I clicked on it, a text bubble opened up: *According to the National Oceanic and Atmospheric Administration (NOAA), humidity levels above 50% and dew points higher than 65° F are deemed uncomfortably high.*

Wow. I hoped *that* wasn't another bad omen for the summer.

I heard Tiara & Co. before I saw them: three figures on the steps of the Town Hall. Mina leaned against the base of the Miss Liberty statue, poking at her phone; Stevie sat on the steps, looking half asleep. Tiara stood on the Town Hall front porch, striking a superhero pose: feet apart and hands on her hips. Two lights that were gunky with dead bugs glowed from the ceiling, and there was a fan that never stopped spinning.

"Finally," Tiara said when she saw me. "You didn't tell anyone you were coming here, right? Not Levi?"

"No."

"Good. I want this to be a surprise. We're going to do what my mom and Levi can't. We're going to make people fall in love with the parade all over again."

We gathered in a circle. I put my shoebox in the middle and removed the lid. Photos and clippings documenting my sister's time in the Liberty Line overflowed the confines of the box. Tiara pulled out a manila envelope and shook out some photos and a newspaper clipping. Mina had a small collection she'd brought in a ziplock baggie while Stevie just tossed down a handful of photos printed on computer paper.

"Jeez, Savvy. You really *are* obsessed," Stevie muttered.

"I prefer the word *passionate*," I retorted as primly as I could.

Tiara spread my photos out on the floorboards. "This is good, Savvy. These go way back. Now, we're going to cover—and I mean *cover*—this entire front wall with these photos. Like an inspiration board."

"Wait—" Mina began. "Isn't this vandalism?"

"No," Tiara stated, handing us each a roll of tape. "We're just reminding everyone how awesome the Miss Liberty parade is."

At first we went slowly, carefully taping the images to the wall. But eventually we all slipped into a zone and couldn't put them up fast enough. I thought about what Dulce had proposed with her historical reflection. It felt like that's what we were doing, only we were doing it on the part of Town Hall that faced the street. Our boldness made me feel like I was naturally daring; no one could deny that there was something very cool about seeing the history of Miss Liberty spread out where everyone could see it. It was like every Miss Liberty was saying *Hellooooo! Don't forget us. We're still here, and we're still important!*

I was trying to center a photo of my sister when red and blue flashes started bouncing off the walls. I whipped around just as a police car pulled up.

"Someone called the cops?" Stevie asked, dumbfounded.

There was a half second of silence. Then Tiara shrieked, "Run!"

Stevie, Mina, and Tiara scattered, racing to the back deck, where there was a second set of stairs. As for me, well, sometimes anxiety makes me move superfast and sometimes it makes me freeze. At this moment, I was frozen.

I could only turn back toward the walls and stare at

what we'd done. To see so many images scrapbooking the exterior of our Town Hall made me feel . . . accomplished.

"All right, drop whatever is in your hand and—wait, Savvy, is that you?"

"Uh . . ."

My weather watch buzzed on my wrist. A red and violet cloud pulsed on the screen, a warning that there was a thirty percent chance of thunderstorms. I glanced at the sky but saw nothing. Shame. I'd kill for a thunderstorm right now.

"We got a call that someone—or someones—was defacing Town Hall. You mind telling us what's going on?"

I looked down the length of the porch, but I was all alone. I couldn't find my voice. The flashing lights were illuminating the Miss Liberty statue and my face, spotlighting us at the same time.

It wasn't the spotlight that I wanted.

10

"I'm trying to decide if I'm annoyed or mad," Glammy drawled.

The AC at the police station shuddered as it blasted North Pole air into a room where everything seemed to be made of linoleum and metal.

"Am I annoyed by the fact that I was woken up from a very deep sleep in the middle of the night by a call saying my granddaughter was at the police station? Or am I mad? I know at one point I was scared out of my mind, but once I was assured you weren't hurt, it made room for other emotions."

"Sorry," I muttered, looking at my watch. The thunderstorm warning had passed. Darn.

"All right." Officer Catana sat down. "I talked to Mayor

Radnor. He's not going to fine her for vandalism—as long as she does some community service."

Glammy stifled a yawn and hitched an elbow over her chair. "Using Scotch tape to put up a bunch of photos is hardly vandalism. I mean, I drove by on my way here. You can hardly see them from the street."

"You can't?" I asked. I guess all that work was for nothing.

"Cleo," Officer Catana began. "Your granddaughter was taping pictures onto a building that's on the National Register of Historic Places. Such an act can be considered vandalism and can constitute a thousand-dollar fine."

"*What?*" Glammy and I cried at the same time.

He nodded. "Yep. So, community service is not that bad. It's up to you to figure out what it is. I know there is highway cleanup along old Route 38, and reading with—"

"She can volunteer with me at Nifty Thrifty!" Glammy cried, clapping her hands together.

I glared at her. She looked so happy. Two seconds ago, she was acting like community service was a bother, and now her eyes were all lit up.

Officer Catana double-clicked his pen before checking off a box. "That works."

"Wait." I sat up straighter. "I can't volunteer, Glammy. I have Miss Liberty rehearsals. And performances! This is my busiest summer *ever*."

"Honey, we'll work around it. I know your schedule. We live together, remember?" She poked me in the side, trying to make me laugh, but I refused. How did my day go from my very first performance to me getting busted and put on mandatory volunteer duty?

So far, I was not having the Glitter Season that I wanted.

11

Dulce and Seymour showed up at my house at ten the next morning.

"You were busted last night!" Dulce cried, aghast.

"How did you hear?"

"Officer Sullivan bumped into my dad getting coffee," she explained. "He said you were arrested! So I went and got Seymour and now we want the whole story."

"Not arrested," Glammy corrected, coming into my room with a basket of laundry. "Savvy was *detained*."

"You can still do parade stuff, right?" Seymour asked.

"Of course she can," Glammy answered for me. "And Savvy's punishment isn't a punishment at all. She's going to be my helper at Nifty Thrifty. But fear not, I'll work around the sacred Liberty schedule. Speaking of, you all have that performance at Shuckey's Arcade at eight tonight. If anyone needs me to wash something, let me know now."

"I'm good," I said. Seymour nodded.

When she swept out of the room, Dulce eyed my pile of newly deposited clean clothes. "Didn't she just do laundry?"

"Glammy likes to do it every single day," I replied. "I think it's a quirk of anxiety, but she won't listen, even though I *am* an expert on the subject."

"Nah, your grandmother is the chillest person I know," Seymour countered, pulling a bag from his backpack and removing swatches of gold and bronze fabric that he started to line up on the bed.

Dulce rapped her pen on her clipboard. "Your pictures are still hanging at Town Hall."

"Yeah, but according to Glammy, you can hardly see them from the road," I grumbled. "Hey, Dulce, I figured you could use them for the reflection thing you were writing, but then I thought . . ."

"What?"

"I don't know . . . they're fun to look at, but they're not doing anything as far as the parade is concerned. I basically told Bobbi I'd help her in any way I could, but I feel like people need a really *heavy* dose of nostalgia. Something bigger than big, or at least bigger than a website."

"*Bigger* than *History Fits?*" Dulce said.

I couldn't tell if she was insulted.

"How would you make it bigger?" Seymour asked.

"No idea."

Glammy swung open the door again. "Savvy, I'm running some errands. Try to avoid criminal activity until I get back."

"I'm not the one with a history of protesting. That's you and Levi."

"You protested?" Seymour asked.

Glammy lifted her chin proudly. "The Great Dior Protest of 1966."

"Great Dior protest?" Dulce asked, pulling out her phone.

"Yes," Glammy said. "It was—"

"Found it!" Dulce called, triumphant. She turned her phone so we could all see.

"Look! There I am!" Glammy cried.

Filling Dulce's screen was a black-and-white photo of Glammy. She looked about Levi's age in the picture. She and a few other women were wearing miniskirts and carrying protest signs. Glammy's sign said *Fight the Patriarchy! Miniskirts Forever!* Another woman had a sign that read *Support the Youth! Support the Miniskirt!*

"Look at the stems on me," Glammy cooed, her voice wistful. "You're not the only tap dancer in the family, Sav."

"Stems?" Dulce asked.

"Legs," Seymour supplied.

"Why is it called the Dior protest?" Dulce asked next.

"Dior is a French luxury line, founded by Christian Dior," Seymour supplied.

Glammy nodded. "In 1966, there was a protest outside a Dior fashion show in London because it didn't feature any miniskirts, which everyone felt was an insult to teenagers. So we decided to launch a 'sister' protest here in the States."

"Did it happen near Fashion Mart?" Seymour asked. A beat, and then, "I bet it happened near Fashion Mart."

Fashion Mart was a thrift-store-meets-garage-sale for old Broadway and movie costumes; all the proceeds went to organizations that helped the homeless. Seymour was always on its website, begging his mom to buy him a sequined hat from *A Chorus Line* or a prop can of hairspray from *Hairspray*.

"Whoa! You're quoted," Dulce continued. "You said, 'When a fashion designer ignores the youth, then I guess we have to demand to be seen and heard in the biggest and loudest way possible. Nothing says big and loud like a protest in New York City.'"

"That is so fierce!" Seymour gasped, grabbing the phone. "Savvy, the women in your family are so fierce."

Glammy grinned. "The best part was talking to people who were genuinely curious about why we were protesting. Such fun conversations." She shook her head like she was shaking off raindrops. "Alrighty, enough reminiscing. I gotta run." Blowing kisses, she was back out the door.

"So, so, so fierce," Seymour declared.

"Is that your word of the day or something?" Dulce asked.

"Of the summer."

"I can be fierce," I insisted.

They looked like they didn't believe me. Not that I blamed them. I didn't really believe it myself.

12

During the school year, Tuesday evenings aren't anything special.

But they are when it's summer and you're a Miss Liberty dancer and you have a night performance to do.

Believe me when I say that performing after the sun goes down makes a person feel sophisticated and adult. You're part of a different world, one where only professionals and die-hard dancers exist.

Oh, and the writers who cover them.

As we left the house, Dulce hugged her clipboard to her chest and drummed her fingers on the back. She always did that when she was thinking.

"I hope I get another good story out of tonight. I'm on a roll with my Miss Liberty series."

"Oh, crud," Seymour cried a second later. "I forgot a water bottle. Let's stop by the bodega."

Everyone else in town just called the store that Seymour's parents owned "the store." But apparently, in New York City, little neighborhood stores were called bodegas. Seymour was obsessed with all things New York, so to him, his parents owned a bodega, *not* a store.

I looked up at the clock that was catty-corner from Town Hall. It read seven thirty, which meant that we had about a half hour.

"Let's hurry," I said.

When we got there and swung the door open, the bodega AC hit us like a melting snow cone.

"Welcome to Lady Liberty Land," Dulce sang.

The entire store was a homage to Miss Liberty, and I *looooved* it. Between pocket packets of tissues, shoe inserts, and road atlases were shelves stocked with Statue of Liberty miniatures, Barbies in the traditional Miss Liberty uniform, and patriotic garden gnomes with star-studded hats. There were also Fourth of July wreaths and American Flag Air Dancers; there were red, white, and blue buntings for the porch, beer belts, earrings, skinny jeans, and welcome mats that said *You Look Like You Need a Fourth of July Break*.

"Hello, chickadees," Mrs. Bardot called, popping up from behind the counter wearing a bucket hat with a red, white, and blue pinwheel. "You were all on fire at the car wash! I'm sorry more people didn't show up."

"Thanks, Mom. Anyone else need water?" Seymour called, heading toward the back fridge.

Dulce and I shook our heads.

Mrs. Bardot came around the counter, smiling at me. "Heard you—*ahem*—*decorated* our Town Hall last night," she teased.

"Wasn't just her," Dulce sang, picking up a Miss Liberty bobblehead.

"It was for a good cause," I said. "We're reminding people about the parade's importance. You're going to Bobbi's luncheon on the fifth, right, Mrs. Bardot? To help show the Town Council that we're serious about keeping the parade here?"

"I suppose I might, but, well . . . I'm not sure a luncheon is going to make a difference. Same with Levi's protest. They're both lovely gestures, but it's too late to stop what's been put into motion. It seems silly to even try."

Silly to even try? Didn't Seymour's mom care about what was going to happen to the parade? How many adults thought like this?

"I think the dancers are lining up!" Mrs. Bardot said, pointing out the window. The street and sidewalk in front of Shuckey's Arcade were blocked off with folding chairs and orange cones. Sure enough, our fellow dancers were gathering near the table where Bobbi had stacked her speakers.

The three of us headed outside, and Seymour and I

joined our fellow dancers on the sidewalk. The arcade's exterior was ablaze with lights, drenching us in neon.

I took my place in line just as Tiara hurried to stand in front of me. She didn't even turn around to apologize for ditching me. In fact, she didn't acknowledge me at all. Anger rumbled in my belly.

"In just a minute we're going to get started!" Bobbi shouted.

Even though the arcade was closed for our performance, "Puttin' on the Ritz" was playing over its speakers. Without thinking, I began to tap my feet.

"Savvy, stand still," Tiara hissed over her shoulder.

I clenched my teeth and kept tapping. "*Don't* boss me around."

Tiara ignored me. I did a shuffle ball step, letting my foot slip to kick her behind her knee.

She whipped around. "Hey! What's your problem?"

"*My* problem? How about *you* ditched me and I got taken to the police station and you're acting like nothing happened? How's that for 'problem'?"

Tiara rolled her shoulders to adjust her posture, emphasizing that she was an inch taller than me. "I'm . . . sorry about that. But you could have run, too."

"You could have come back."

"Puttin' on the Ritz" kept playing on a loop. Just as it was starting over again, Bobbi walked over to me. Pretending to fix my ponytail, she leaned low. "*Where* is Levi?"

"I don't know. She should be here."

"Mom, she's right over . . ." Tiara's voice trailed off. I followed her gaze toward the right of our staging area. There was Levi, wearing a tux. Not the Miss Liberty costume. *A tux.*

My aunt inhaled sharply, her breath practically whistling through her teeth.

As soon as people saw my sister, the phones came out. I couldn't tell how many there were exactly, but I guessed at least thirty, plus the camera crews from Channel 3 and Channel 4, who had their lenses trained on Levi.

Levi took center stage, positioning herself directly in front of the moving lights of the arcade. "Everyone, welcome to another Miss Liberty performance!" She extended her arms out in a V. "We are thrilled to continue the countdown to our famous, historic parade. And, as your Miss Liberty—your glamorous symbol of freedom—I would like to encourage everyone to ask themselves if moving the Liberté voting location is a reflection of equality or a sign of disenfranchisement. If you are unhappy with the fact that the voting location has moved farther away, please join me for the protest that is still scheduled to take place on July fifth. This protest is our chance to—"

The music suddenly blasted, cutting Levi off. Looking over at the speakers, I saw that my aunt wore a tight smile as she turned a knob to increase the volume.

Levi rolled with it, and we all performed our dance as

usual. Still, something felt off. Not everyone hit the body pops at the same time, and for the fan kick ripple, some of us—me included—could barely get our legs up. Even though I'd stretched, my tendons felt like rubber bands with no elasticity.

"That tux is cursing us," Tiara hissed.

Finally, Levi did her spinning magic right there on the sidewalk, a blur of tuxedo tails and white sneakers. When she hit her final pose, the rest of us hustled forward to take a bow. The crowd clapped, but it wasn't the roar of applause I was dying for.

"Bobbi!" It was Gwen from Channel 4. I knew her because she always wore a shade of lipstick that was the color of Cheetos. "The Miss Liberty costume has been worn since 1952 and was based on the original 1920 costume. Why switch it up tonight?"

"Well—" Bobbi began, struggling to keep her smile as she stood next to Levi. "If you see the same costume all the time, it loses its special quality."

"How is the town coping with the loss of the parade?" shouted a reporter with the letters WHNY on his mic. It was the public radio station Dulce talked about working for someday.

"*Potential* loss, Don," Bobbi corrected. "Don't believe every rumor you hear, please. This parade isn't dead and buried. In fact, if you all haven't heard, *I'll* be hosting a luncheon on July fifth to officially resurrect the Miss Liberty parade with a petition and small-town spirit. Our Town Council won't be able to ignore pages and pages of signatures."

"I just figured it out," Seymour whispered. "Your sister looks like a spy. A femme fatale spy."

"She looks like a chauffeur," Tiara quipped.

"July fifth?" Gwen asked. "That's the same day as the Miss Liberty protest. Are you two in competition?"

Levi and Bobbi just glanced at each other, then looked away.

"*Awk-ward*," sang Stevie.

Bobbi laughed tactfully. "Oh, stop. Miss Liberty and I are always in sync."

"This is a question for Levi," the WHNY reporter called out again. "Are you getting bored with the Miss Liberty title? Is that the reason for the costume switch-up?"

Levi straightened the lapels on her jacket. "Not bored. I've just come to believe that Miss Liberty should be doing more—taking action and talking to people, encouraging everyone to take a stand when our freedoms are being chipped away. As a figurehead and symbol for freedom, Miss Liberty's voice should be the loudest of all."

"But Miss Liberty doesn't talk," someone shouted from the back of the crowd. For some reason, that made people laugh.

Levi smiled. "She does *now*."

"But how does the tuxedo fit into Miss Liberty taking a stand on issues?" Gwen nudged.

While Bobbi had her pearls in a choke hold, Levi took a step forward. "When I'm in the Miss Liberty costume, I have to behave a certain way, smile pretty and be silent. I figure that if I step out of the Miss Liberty costume every once in a while, I can shake off those restrictions." She paused, then added with a smile full of sass, "Anyway, I think I look good in a tux."

Bobbi released her pearls. "Alrighty, everyone, let's get to the fun part of the night. The arcade will now reopen. Enjoy!"

She bowed again, took Levi by the elbow, and pulled her into the bodega.

While most dancers ran for the arcade, Tiara, Stevie, Mina, Seymour, and I stayed put, watching Levi and Bobbi through the window.

"I wish I could read lips," I muttered.

"Excuse me, aren't you Levi Montrose's little sister? Savvy, right?"

I turned around and almost passed out. Gwen Marlon was looking directly at me, her cameraman behind her.

"What? Oh . . . hello. Yes. I'm Savvy."

Gwen smiled. "Do you have a second? I was just wondering about the tux. I know it seems like we're focused on that, but I've covered this parade for six years now, and Miss Liberty has never rocked the boat like this. When a person sees the Miss Liberty costume, they don't associate it with dissent."

Tiara stepped forward. "You should probably talk to my mom. Savvy really isn't in the know. In fact—"

"I know my sister has a lot on her mind," I interrupted, glaring at my cousin. "She's . . . um . . . worried about voting. Or about where we vote. Not me. I can't vote yet. And I know she wants to draw attention to . . . um . . . the place, the *voting* place, but, well, I guess she's a little all over the place and . . . but she'll be fine for the parade. Is Yvette coming to the parade?"

"Yvette Rayne? Probably. So you're saying that your sister is a little scattered?"

"Uh . . ."

Dulce cleared her throat. "Excuse me, Gwen, but, as the *historian* of Liberté, I think it's worth noting that traditionally, when women appear in tuxedos, it's seen as a sign of defying cultural norms."

Gwen wrote that down. "Interesting."

"Is it, though?" Mina asked dryly.

Gwen turned toward her cameraman. "We've got enough for now, Tony. Let's get back to Philly."

Tiara chastised me the second Gwen was out of earshot. "You shouldn't have spoken to her, Savvy."

"I had to say something."

"That's it. It's Pac-Man time," Stevie announced. "Who's with me?"

Tiara and Mina followed Stevie into the arcade, but Dulce shook her head. "I need to get writing. See you guys later."

"Okay." Seymour looked at me. "Savvy, you coming? Skee-Ball?"

"Um, sure. I'll be just a second."

Honestly, I didn't feel like going into the noisy arcade. Even standing outside, the buzzing and electric whizzes were echoing in my skull.

Too much noise, too much light, too much clutter, too much thinking. Was I going to be in trouble for talking to Gwen? I didn't say anything wrong, did I? And is there a way to save Miss Liberty by getting people to remember the importance of our town's history?

I watched Bobbi and my sister exit the bodega; then Bobbi headed back to the remaining reporters and parents, all smiles and charm. Levi, however, put her hands in her pockets and walked in the opposite direction toward home. She didn't even look back, so I just kept watching her move away from all the lights, letting the night swallow her in one gulp.

13

Mrs. Bardot gave me a ride home. When I came inside the house, I noticed that Glammy was on the phone, but Levi was nowhere in sight.

"Is that Mom and Dad?" I asked.

Glammy shook her head. "Sorry. Nifty Thrifty call. Eliza thinks it's great that you'll be helping out."

"Super," I muttered. "Does she know I'm being forced?"

Glammy just waved a hand at me, so I wandered out to the deck, where Levi was sitting. She was still in her tuxedo, her bare feet propped up on the railing, her mango-painted toenails especially bright under the deck lights. Next to her, a cigar sat in an ashtray that was shaped like a napping iguana.

"You're *smoking*?"

"The cigar fits my look. I found it in Grandpa's old stash."

"Fits your *look*? You mean the suit that I'm pretty sure you stole from Dad's closet?"

"A performer uses what is at her disposal."

I saw her iPad on her lap. "What are you reading?"

"The Constitution."

"Seriously?"

"Yep."

I plopped down in the chair next to her, kicking off my shoes, and put my feet up too. I could see my bare toes through the tan spandex of my tights. I wondered if Levi would let me use her nail polish.

"Everyone in town is talking about you," I said. "Even reporters are asking questions."

"Good."

"*Good*?" I just stared at the cigar. The smell was making me dizzy. And thirsty.

Levi picked it up and waved it before her like it was a wand. "*Saxum suffragio*," she declared.

"Sax . . . saxum . . . what?"

"*Saxum suffragio*. It means—well, at least I think it means—rock the vote in Latin. Saying 'rock the vote' in plain old English was popular in the 1990s. It was used to try to get young people excited to vote."

"Ah." I nodded as if I understood everything she was saying, when really I was confused as to why we were discussing things people said way back in the 1990s.

"I was messing around with online translations. My civics teacher said that if you don't vote, you don't have the right to complain." She sagged deeper into the chair. I waited for the wicker to break. "I don't want to wear the tux again. I need a new look to keep people talking. No one asks questions when I'm wearing the costume they expect me to wear. They see the Miss Liberty outfit and they think, 'Oh, look. *It's the same old Miss Liberty. She's going to smile and say nothing and be our little mascot of happy American pride.*' Well, I'm not happy just smiling and saying nothing. I want people to care about something *big*."

She tapped her screen and angled it toward me. "What do you think?"

I immediately recognized the picture she had pulled up. We had studied it when looking at images of World War II in history class last year. Mrs. Ferris had spent a couple of days talking about how art and advertisements were used to get people on the home front to support those fighting in the war. My favorite image had been the one my sister was showing me now: Rosie the Riveter, a woman wearing a red polka-dot handkerchief in her hair, her denim shirtsleeve rolled up to reveal a perfect muscle.

"You can take one look at her and understand that she's serious about supporting America!" Mrs. Ferris had said.

"That's Rosie," I told Levi. "Rosie the Riveter."

"Exactly," Levi whispered in awe. "But actually, I like this depiction of her better."

She swiped the screen and a new photo popped up. This

time, Rosie wore overalls and had even bigger muscles. She had bright red hair and a sandwich in one hand. "This is Rosie by Norman Rockwell."

"What's she eating? Pastrami?"

Levi shook her head. "No way. Definitely ham and cheese. Swiss cheese."

"Ew. Gross."

"Okay. Fine. Not Swiss. It's that fancy cheese that we used to get 'cause Dad liked it. Hav-hav—"

"Havarti!" I cried.

"That's the one. That was really good cheese."

"I love cheese."

Levi nodded. "Best food there is."

For some reason, all the talk about cheese had us both giggling, as if we hadn't just been talking about serious things.

Fireflies fluttered past our toes; I wished I could hold on to this moment. I pretended that these seconds were going to stretch through the entire summer and beyond. Since I was pretending, I went ahead and pretended that right now, my sister was marveling at how cool and mature I was, and because I was so cool and mature, we'd keep talking until three in the morning and then we'd creep back into the house and she'd show me how to do a real French manicure and how to apply fake lashes so they blended seamlessly with my lash line.

Instead, Levi broke the moment by standing up. "Good night, Sav. Thanks for your help."

"I didn't do anything."

"You let me babble. Think out loud. That's always helpful. Good night." She blew me a kiss and practically danced inside. She was so chipper I half expected to see glitter swirling in her wake.

I wondered what it would be like to be that chipper, to go to bed without a single worry clogging your brain. I'd probably never know.

That night, I dreamed about my third-grade cancan dance number, the one where we had to shake and shimmy our shoulders so much that it made my teeth vibrate. Then I realized someone was actually shaking my shoulders, trying to wake me up.

"Savvy, open your eyes. You'll miss your morning news debut."

Levi was sitting on my bed, glaring at me. Gone was the sister from last night. She had her laptop with her, open to the Channel 4 news page and paused on one of the morning anchors, Chad. He was the one with radioactive blond hair and an intense smile that showed off teeth as big as dominoes.

The time read 6:11 a.m. "Why am I looking at the news?" I said groggily.

"Oh, just watch."

She hit the space bar and suddenly there I was, in front of Shuckey's Arcade!

"Let's revisit our footage from last night," Chad said, "when Gwen checked out the performance that was part of the lead-up to Liberté's famous and historic Fourth of July parade."

"Only parade like it in the state," his coanchor said.

"This is Savvy Montrose, sister of Levi Montrose—Miss Liberty for three years running. Although this town is preparing to say goodbye to its parade, Miss Liberty seems ready to go out with a bang as she eschews the traditional Miss Liberty costume for her own outfits."

It cut away from me to Levi performing in her tux. Then I was on the screen again and Gwen was speaking: "When asked about why her sister is being footloose and fancy-free with the costuming, Savvy Montrose had a telling reply."

To my horror, I heard my voice next: "She's a little all over the place."

"What?" I cried. "I didn't *just* say that. I said a lot of other stuff. I said there are things that are important to you. I mentioned voting . . . and, and—"

Levi snapped her laptop shut. "It doesn't matter what else you say. You gave them a sound bite. You said that I'm 'all over the place.' You know what that means? It means that people can say that I'm hysterical or unfocused or . . . that I'm just some dumb teenager who doesn't understand how voting and politics work. Don't speak for me, Savvy, *okay?*"

She got up and headed for the door. I noticed that she

was wearing her Fourth of July boxers, the ones Mom got her, with the fireworks and the words *boom*, *pow*, *crash*, and *pop* all over them.

Before I could say anything else, she slammed my bedroom door so hard that even Bert flinched.

14

When I walked into the dance studio later that day, I was still bothered by my TV snippet with Gwen. Had Bobbi seen it? Was I going to be in trouble? Why had Gwen used only part of what I'd said? The one time I say anything—and it was all messed up.

Tiara, Mina, and Stevie were huddled in the front of the room, near the record player. (We were one of the few dance studios that still had a record player.)

"Look at what they're wearing," Seymour whispered, resting an elbow on my shoulder and using his other hand to wave a red and black silk fan. "They've always got the fashionable stuff. The *chic* stuff."

"Chic?"

"Another word for 'fashionable.' You learn a lot of great

vocab when your mom gets you a *Vogue* subscription for your birthday."

"Of course."

He wasn't wrong. Tiara & Co. were dressed like professional dancers. While the rest of us were still in tan tights, black leotards, and jazz sneakers, they looked like those dancer/model hybrids from *Divine Dance Magazine*, with their cropped sweaters, sweatshirts with the collars cut off, and mismatched leg warmers.

Seymour and I sat down to stretch.

"Did you see me on the news?" I reluctantly asked.

He nodded. "It was one silly sentence. I wouldn't worry about it. Is Levi mad?"

"She thinks I made her look dumb and scattered."

Bobbi marched out of the office, clapping a 1–2–3-and-a-1–2–3 staccato to draw our attention. We clapped back at the same rhythm.

"Before we begin, I need to say something." She paused and scanned the room. "You know what? Let's all hold hands."

"Since when do we hold hands?" Seymour whispered.

Once we were all holding hands in an egg-shaped circle, Bobbi took a deep breath. "Let's call this our sacred, get-on-the-same-page moment. We have about two weeks until the parade. I know everyone thinks it will be the last one, but so help me, as long as there is breath in my body, I refuse to believe that. But I need everyone's support.

We are a *team*. That means we function as a unit. *No one* talks to reporters without me, and *no one* operates with an agenda. Miss Liberty has always been a beacon of American pride. People feel better when they look at her. She's a *positive* role model with her perfect dance steps and perfect smiles. When you all perform on July Fourth, I need your performance to light up the entire town."

As she spoke, Bobbi's eyes glanced from Stevie to Seymour, skipping over me, as if we were playing a game of duck, duck, goose and she didn't want to touch my head.

"Now I'd like everyone to stretch before we get started. Savvy, I need to speak with you."

"Um, Bobbi—" Seymour called, rising and hurrying to his bag. "Can I show you something first?"

"I'll look at your fans later, Seymour."

"Oh, thank you, but no. I just wanted to show you the sketches for a costume I've been working on." He fumbled in his bag, pulling out his sketchbook, stray feathers escaping as he did so. "I was thinking we needed a costume that was even bolder than the usual. So, I've been—"

"Later, Seymour, I promise," Bobbi called, putting her hand on my back to gently steer me into her office. She closed the door behind us.

The first thing my aunt said to me was this: "Savvy, I think you and I are more alike than anyone else in the family. It's probably why I trust you completely."

"You do?" My heart accelerated like I had just chugged

three energy drinks in a row. *This was fantastic!* I thought I was going to get in trouble, but to hear my aunt say that she trusted me completely?

Bobbi nodded. "You believe in this parade as it has always existed. Just like me. And you believe that Miss Liberty is a special figure who should reign just as she's always reigned. I'll concede that we could maybe spice things up a bit with slight changes. *Slight.* Maybe we could add a silver panel to your skirts or bows to your character shoes. Maybe you could wave as you come onstage or—"

"*Or* maybe we could add a new dance, like a tap dance. If not this year, then maybe next year."

"*See!*" Bobbi slapped her hands on her knees, causing me to jump. "I love your optimism! That's also why we're alike. We both know that this parade will still be *here* next year. We just have to deliver the magic, like we always do. Make people remember how their best summer memories are of the parade."

"Absolutely," I agreed, slapping my own knees. Finally, I was having a conversation with someone who saw things as clearly as I did. "We use nostalgia."

"Also," Bobbi continued, "I understand that your comment to Gwen on this morning's news was probably taken out of context, so let's just put that in the 'learning' column and forget about it. I really do rely on you and your dedication. I'm guessing you were as blindsided by the tux as I was, so I need to know: Is Levi going to be wearing the *appropriate* costume from this point on? We still have the Honeybee Fair and the show."

I gulped. My lips were dry. My throat was dry. I recalled the way my sister had looked at Rosie the Riveter. Should I say something about that? But what was there to say?

The only answer I could give Bobbi was "Yes. For sure."

Bobbi leaned back in her chair and started twisting her pearls. "You're completely sure?"

"Totally and completely sure."

"Wonderful." She patted her pearls like she was trying to comfort them. "I actually feel bad for Levi. She's trying to force this voting agenda down people's throats. No one is going to show up for her protest. There's nothing *to* protest. So the voting location has moved. So what? It's a minor inconvenience." She shook her head. "Thank you, Savvy. Head back into the studio and stretch."

It wasn't until much later that I realized that Bobbi had never said anything about my tap solo.

15

Two hours later, I was entering Nifty Thrifty, inhaling what smelled like stale saltines, lavender, and lemon polish.

"Oh, here's my little helper!" Glammy hurried over. She hugged me, then turned to face two older ladies standing at the counter. "Eliza, Camilla, you remember my granddaughter Savvy."

I recognized them from picking up Glammy when they were all heading to the outlets or going to play pickleball. Eliza always wore ginormous hoops, and Camilla had frosted blond curls that she teased high above her head.

"Savvy! Hello!" Eliza called. "Glad to get some young blood in here to help out."

Nifty Thrifty had everything from clothing to footwear

to jewelry to appliances to knickknacks. The knickknack category included trinkets—like porcelain angels with wicked smiles, vintage sewing kit travel boxes, belt buckles, and pillows that looked uncomfortable on account of layers of lace.

Glammy steered me through racks of winter coats and rain jackets to a back corner where there were boxes and laundry bins full of donations.

"I need you to go through these and divide them into categories. Sorry you have to sit on the floor. The mayor bought the one decent folding table that we had left. Said he'd been looking for a table that was the perfect height so he can run his projector for the parade. You know anything about that?"

"No."

"He said he and Bobbi decided that he's going to project images of flags waving on the back wall of the stage area."

"I'm surprised Bobbi didn't say anything to me. She and I are basically a team now." If it sounded like I was bragging, it's because I was.

"Are you all talking about what the mayor's got planned?" Eliza asked, dumping a box on the floor beside me. I saw a bunch of towels and one freaky porcelain clown with a cantaloupe slice of a grin. "Did you know he just has to plug his phone into the projector, and that's how he'll transmit those images to the backdrop? We're in the land of sophisticated technology!" She pointed at the first box.

"So, anyway, shoes obviously go with shoes, and dresses with dresses, but people donate miscellaneous stuff. Anything remotely fancy—like jewelry—we like to put in the display case up front, so you can set them aside. Have fun! Holler if you need anything."

Glammy kissed me on the head, and she and Eliza left me to the mess.

I thought of all the things I could be doing *instead of* this: working on tap dancing, or practicing mindfulness exercises, or seeing if Bobbi needed an assistant.

"I would be a great assistant," I said aloud.

I settled down before the first box. It was easy to organize because it was just full of quilts. Next was a box that was full of . . . *Fourth of July decorations?* Who was getting rid of their Fourth of July decorations?

"Hey, Sav."

I turned around and saw Dulce coming in, carrying a box.

"Hi! What are you doing here?"

"Dad has secretly started getting rid of Mom's eighteen thousand purses. He asked me to donate them. I told him that's just going to make her want to buy more, but he didn't listen. Your Glammy said I could set them here."

"Yeah, yeah, right here." I scooted over and peered into the box as Dulce plunked it down. I saw a brown and olive green handbag made of what looked like scales. "Is this from a real alligator?"

Dulce nodded, giving me a wide-eyed, horrified look. She eyed the few piles I had made. "This is actually pretty cool, as far as punishments go. I bet there are some treasures buried here."

"You mean like *these*?" I held up a pair of the shiniest loafers I had ever seen: licorice-red with pointy toes and heels that weren't even scuffed. Shoving my hands into the shoes, I clapped them together so that the heels clattered and echoed.

"Put them on!" Dulce said.

Giggling, I kicked off my sneakers and put on the fancy shoes. Of course they were too big, but I was still able to stand and do a toe-heel-toe-heel walk. I did a shuffle next. "I can turn anything into tap shoes."

Dulce clasped her hand in mock prayer. "A true gift."

A second later we heard Glammy's voice yelling from the front. "We're working *while* we're playing, right girls?"

"Yes!" we called.

I plopped back down on the floor, lifted my legs and clicked my toes together. "I tried to talk to Bobbi about doing a tap solo, but she didn't really hear me. She just wants me to warn her if Levi is going to do anything else."

"Incoming!" Glammy called, coming around with a small box. "Mayor Radnor's assistant just dropped these off. Said they're part of a stash of pictures that had been kept in the storage room at Town Hall."

"He's getting rid of pictures?" Dulce asked. "But . . . this is history."

"Apparently most are duplicates. The really important ones were filed. The town just doesn't have the storage space. You know someone is going to want them."

The minute Glammy walked away, Dulce and I popped open the lid. There were piles of black-and-white photos, sepia-toned photos, and full-blown color photos. They weren't in any kind of order. A photo with the year 1977 written on the back was in the same folder as a picture of a girl in a red, white, and blue ensemble holding a sign that read *Happy Fourth of July from the Class of 1989*.

I pulled out a photo of a Miss Liberty I didn't recognize. I guessed it was from the 1950s, because her hair was in a ponytail that was flipped at the end and her bangs were a perfect shelf.

"Wow. Check this out. It's Bobbi," Dulce said, holding up a picture. Sure enough, there was Bobbi, perched on a float that was covered in American flags. "I forgot Miss Liberty used to have a float in the parade."

I found another photo of dancers in sparkly red leotards with blue tulle skirts. The photo was taken from an angle that let us see the crowds.

"I didn't know that many people even *lived* here," I whispered.

"Hey, here's Levi!" Dulce cried. She held up a photo of Levi when she was around the age of thirteen. I could tell because she had braces.

"I think that was her first year in the Liberty Line," I said. Fireworks wallpapered the sky behind her. She was smiling, her hands on her hips. It was obvious—to me, at least—that the girl in the picture was destined for greatness.

We spent almost an hour going through the photos.

"Look at my arms," Dulce said, holding them out. "Goose bumps. That's what history does to me. It's too bad you guys didn't have all these pictures when decorating Town Hall."

I stared at a photo of Levi laughing with Deja and Bobbi. No one was looking at the camera. They were all looking at each other, caught up in the moment.

"I wonder if there's a way to make some kind of display that everyone sees at the same time." I thought back to what I'd said to Dulce and Seymour the morning after Glammy had to pick me up at the police station. "Something bigger than big."

"You've said that. But what do you mean exactly?"

"Like, on this DVD of Marlene Dietrich that Levi, Glammy, and I watched. Before the movie began, it went down memory lane, showing her best clips from other movies."

"Ah, like the highlights. Dad always watches highlights of Super Bowl games," Dulce mused. "I still say I can put photos up on my website; make a slideshow presentation like Mrs. Ferris did when we started a new unit. I've got followers, so I'm kinda big. Big-ish, at least."

"A slideshow might work," I agreed. "*Or*, wouldn't it be cool if we could make a commercial or something, have it appear after Yvette gives her weather report?" I was already laying photos out side by side, swapping them like I was a Tarot card reader trying to ensure the best fortune.

"Nice storyboard, Savvy," Dulce said, complimenting me when I finished lining up the first dozen.

I sat back on my haunches. "Thanks. I think we should call it the Greatest Hits of Miss Liberty!"

Dulce handed me more photos, and I found places for all of them. Before long, the storyboard for Miss Liberty's Greatest Hits stretched from the shoe rack to the dressers, almost the length of a lane at the Liberté Bowling Alley.

"This is going to be a *long* slideshow," Dulce observed.

I nodded. "A long slideshow for an epic parade."

What I didn't say was that Dulce's website still didn't feel grand enough for any kind of slideshow. I wanted everyone in town to see these images all at the same time, to be unable to look away, to study the story of Miss Liberty until they felt so mushy and weepy and sentimental about the parade that they would agree to never, ever let it go.

16

And then, it was the night of our Honeybee Fair performance, the second most important show we would be doing that summer. The fair was in Whynot, a neighboring town that had gotten bigger while Liberté had gotten smaller.

We Liberty Line dancers would be wearing our official costumes, which were similar to the Miss Liberty costume. We wore pleated skirts, too, but half of us wore solid blue skirts and the other half wore red skirts. The panels were a mix of foil, lamé, spandex, and cotton. Our leotards were white, decorated with gold seed beads and rhinestones.

Back in May, when I was handed a red skirt, I felt like I had hit the lottery. Red is an exclamation-point color, a look-at-me-quick-before-I-burn-out-all-my-spectacular-energy color.

"Oh, look. Levi remembered her costume." Mina sniffed, pointing to my sister as we took off our oversize cover-ups.

I breathed a sigh of relief as we lined up on the steps that led to the stage in the middle of the fairgrounds. I had been watching my sister carefully at home and had seen no sign of anything Rosie the Riveter.

Scanning the crowd, I saw parents, the usual reporters, and carnival goers. Dulce was front and center with her phone and her clipboard.

Our remix began with the belly-thumping drums of "Sing, Sing, Sing." Thinking of the photos Dulce and I had pored over, I was secretly hoping she would take good photos of me.

Everything felt perfect as I started dancing. My legs kicked higher than usual and my turns were wobble-free. But as we moved into a five-star formation where our hands met in the middle, Seymour's thumb scratched my palm.

"Something's wrong with Levi's costume," he whispered.

Even though Levi was moving fast through her turns, I saw what Seymour was referring to: the back of her leotard was starting to open at the top. Was her zipper broken? My cheeks grew hot, and my breath started sputtering like a rusty sprinkler. Our third performance—the first where we were *all* in costume—and my sister's ensemble was falling apart!

Levi stopped dancing and then swung her arms above

her head. I could tell her costume was gaping open in the back, the teeth of the zipper no longer connecting. Still, that was our cue to encircle her while doing turns of our own. But as we were turning, my sister backed up through a space between Mina and Tiara and raced down the back steps, holding the back of her costume with one hand.

The music continued, and our sequence was done. This was when Levi was supposed to be doing her turns. But where *was* Levi? The question was on Bobbi's face, but all we could do was hold our poses and our smiles and wait.

The crowds waited, too; Levi didn't return. Tiara turned to glare at me. I know what she was thinking: *We all look like we don't know what we're doing!*

That's when I got an idea. Maybe Bobbi hadn't jumped at my tap-dancing solo because she *didn't know how good I was*.

The music shifted, the trombones giving way to drums again. It felt like the stage was vibrating. The music was in my bones, behind my ears, and in that weird spot under my tongue.

So I started to tap, back and forth, right and then left; a spontaneous solo that I couldn't stop. I was essentially faking a routine, making something out of warm-up steps and floorwork sequences.

Some people noticed, but most didn't. I had to be louder. And bigger.

I started to stomp through my taps. Now eyes shifted

to me, including Bobbi's; but she wasn't smiling. Her index finger created a fishhook around her pearls, like she wanted to yank the necklace off.

I shouldn't have locked eyes with her. Once I did, she shook her head. That headshake made the music disappear, turned my muscles into soggy bread. I slowed down my tapping, then stopped cold. Out of the corner of my eye I saw a figure enter from stage right.

It was Levi, wearing head-to-toe denim, her hair twisted up and pinned in the back, a red and white polka-dotted handkerchief wrapped around her head.

Miss Liberty was gone. In her place was Rosie the Riveter.

As Rosie, Levi continued her choreography, performing her signature turns and spins, pausing to blow kisses and waves. With her final turn, she stepped back. Recognizing this part of the choreography, the rest of us shook off our stupor and did our ripple hinge kicks, then dropped our bodies, slowly rolling up and hitting our pose.

The second we did, Levi stepped forward. "Tonight I come to you as Rosie the Riveter. Just as Rosie wanted everyone to do their part during World War II, I'd like to remind *you* all to do your part for democracy. Demand that the Liberté voting location be moved back to its original home! And don't forget the protest that will be held in front of Liberté's Town Hall on July fifth, led by yours truly."

Wearing the biggest smile, Levi blew two kisses at the crowd, turned around sharply, and scampered offstage.

The rest of us just exchanged looks. We managed to bow at the same time before we scuttled offstage. Once we were free, I saw some dancers go off with their parents to enjoy the fair. I started to look for mine, then remembered that they were in Kansas or Colorado, or somewhere west of the Mississippi.

Stevie, Mina, Tiara, and I stayed put, frozen in place to the left of the stairs that led to the stage. We pretended to fix our makeup and pull up our tights, but really we were watching Bobbi and Levi. They were standing on the grass, in front of the stage where everyone could see them.

"I got some great shots of you guys," Dulce said as she joined our gawking circle.

"What is *up* with Levi?" Tiara growled.

"She obviously doesn't care about Miss Liberty anymore." Mina snorted. We all watched as my sister walked away from Bobbi, heading across the fairgrounds to the funnel cake booth.

"That's a bit judgmental," Seymour said.

"Is it?" Mina demanded. "That costume is sacred. Miss Liberty has no business appearing in anything else. It'd be like Miss America appearing onstage without her sash."

"We're calling it a night, everyone!" Bobbi shouted, still in front of the stage. "But, as a reminder, we're only a week and a half away from the big day, and our dancers are only five days away from our annual day trip to New York City. This year, they'll be taking a class at New York Lights Dance Studio and seeing the musical *Contact*. If anyone wants to donate money to help us cover gas expenses for the bus, check out our website. Whoo-hoo!"

"That was the flattest *Whoo-hoo* I've ever heard," Stevie observed. Then she looked at the food tents. "Who wants funnel cake?"

"I can't believe Bobbi just asked for gas money," Tiara grumbled. "We're desperate."

"Hey!" Seymour cried, poking me. "You started doing a solo, Savvy. That was pretty cool."

"Yeah, what was that about?" Mina demanded.

"I think we need a tap number," I meekly muttered. "That's all."

"We need something," Tiara grumbled, still staring at her mom.

17

When I woke up the next day, Sunday, Bert was still sleeping. My brain was totally relaxed. Usually I wake up with a worry or two muscling its way to the front of my mind, but not today.

I had no rehearsals and no Nifty Thrifty duty, so I decided to camp out on the sofa and watch the morning *and* afternoon weekend weather forecasts. Dulce and Seymour were coming over at five for our first official sleepover of the summer. Every year we say we're going to stay up all night (we never do), eat junk food until we puke (never happens), and watch the scariest movies imaginable (the scariest movie we could handle so far has been *Return to* Oz, which, believe me, would freak anyone out).

After watching the weather, I went up to my room to

decorate my weather planner and to write down Yvette's weather word of the day: *exotic lightning*.

I headed downstairs at a quarter to five, ticking off the things we would need for the sleepover: popcorn, of course, and sodas, and probably—

On the bottom step, I froze. Glammy had taken over the living room with her sparkly tiaras.

Usually, the tiaras were at her house, encased in glass cabinets and one converted aquarium, but today, all thirty-two of them were either on the coffee table or perched on cushions and chairs.

She hummed as she polished her pride and joy: a Swarovski pink and citrine diadem that she had worn when she was invited to California to be a Tangerine Queen.

"It's a shame to have these all cooped up at my house," she said, switching crowns and buffing a gem that was as big as a beetle. Then she turned it toward me. "Pop quiz. What type is this?"

I pursed my lips, studying it for a moment. "A bandeau. They look like headbands."

"Very good."

While everyone else learned shapes in preschool, I learned about different types of tiaras. There were diadems, which could be subdivided into wire diadems and beaded diadems. Then there were circlets, which are really similar to corollas, only I think corollas have thicker bands. Then there are headbands, laurel wreaths, and fairy queen flower tiaras.

Since there was nowhere to sit unless I wanted to be lanced with wire and crystals, I plopped down on the floor. Glammy gestured toward the crowns like they were cupcakes she'd just pulled out of the oven.

"Pick one."

"What?"

"I'm serious, Savvy. It's your first Miss Liberty parade, and you deserve a crown."

I immediately reached for the aigrette crown, the one with a fuchsia mohawk and rhinestones the color of fruit punch.

"Ooh, you went right for Miss Tropical Teen. It came with a trip to Hawaii."

"Wow," I breathed. "Crowns get you everything." I let my fingers brush the hot pink spray of feathers, but then I put it down. "No. I haven't earned it. You have to *earn* crowns."

"Nonsense. I think you deserve it."

"Why?"

"No one is as enthusiastic about Miss Liberty as you are. That's deserving, in my book."

"Hell-oo!" I heard Seymour a second before he and Dulce walked into the room. "We didn't think you'd mind if we let ourselves . . ." His voice trailed off and his eyes got huge.

"I knew you were in a lot of beauty pageants and dance competitions," Dulce said to Glammy, "but, whoa!"

"Well, you two are in luck. My collection is cluttering my apartment. So, everyone gets a crown today."

"Are you serious?" Seymour asked, practically drooling.

Dulce shook her head. "But I'm not even in the Liberty Line."

"Doesn't matter. You're the Liberté historian."

Seymour reached for the Miss Memorial Day Crown, a stiff explosion of wires with red, gold, and blue crystals dangling from it like wishes. Biting her lip, Dulce tentatively picked up a diadem made from stones in every shade of blue.

"Miss Siren of the Sea," Glammy breathed. "That was one of my first crowns. Our prom theme was Ocean Fantasy. Now, doesn't everyone feel better?"

"Absolutely!" Seymour declared, eyeing his reflection on the TV screen.

"Thank you," Dulce said. "But can I keep this here? I—I'm not sure I should have anything nice at our house right now."

"Sure," I said. "But why?"

At first Dulce didn't say anything. Then she pulled her legs into her chest and buried her face between her knees. Seymour and I exchanged glances. Dulce wasn't a crier. I think I saw her cry only once, when her pet rat, Rico, died and we buried him in her yard in one of her mom's Prada shoeboxes.

"Our car got repossessed," Dulce growled, the tears evident through her gruffness.

"Oh, honey!" Glammy cried.

I wasn't sure what to say, so I put my arm around her. Seymour put his hand on her knee.

Repossessed. I knew that word. My parents had joked about it when they realized that finances were going to be tight with their new business venture. Repossessed was when someone called a "repo man" seized your car or a lender took your property because you couldn't pay your bills. That's how dad had explained it to me, anyway.

All I knew was that repo man sounded like "bogeyman" and I'm guessing they were equally bad.

Dulce lifted her head, using the heels of her hands to wipe away tears. "I told myself I wouldn't keep feeling upset. Dad's upset enough for the rest of us."

"Sweetie, no one is taking anyone's crown. Not on my watch," Glammy said. "You can keep it here and come get it whenever you want."

I nodded. "Until I become Miss Liberty, I will be the crown keeper."

"Crown keeper," Glammy nodded. "Perfect."

Finally, I had a title.

Because Levi had dressed up as Rosie the Riveter, Dulce said she was in the mood for a World War II movie, specifically one starring Rosie. While we were searching for something that fit the bill, Glammy breezed into the room.

"Alrighty," she called, heading to the stairs. "Levi is

staying overnight at Deja's . . . I guess it's raining at the Shore all week so she came back. Don't turn the TV up too loud please."

"We won't," Seymour and I chorused, just as Dulce said, "Got something! Documentary about the American home front during the war."

About halfway through the documentary, Dulce declared: "Who knew a documentary on factories, welding, and riveting could be so fascinating?"

"How can you tell? You've been on your phone," Seymour teased.

"Who are you texting, anyway?" I asked, lifting my head.

"I'm not texting. I'm messing with those images you picked out for the Miss Liberty slideshow."

"Ooh, can I see?" I begged.

"Just a sec." She glanced up as the documentary showed footage of a factory in New York City. "You guys excited for your New York trip?"

"More than excited," Seymour said. "As long as we get to go to Fashion Mart, of course."

"Of course," I teased, though I doubted Bobbi was going to let us take a side trip.

"Okay. Take a look," Dulce said, handing Seymour her phone so the three of us could see the screen.

"And these are the photos that the mayor's office donated?" Seymour asked.

"Pretty much," I said. "I tried to put them in chronological order, but some didn't have dates, so I had to use hairstyles to guess."

The three of us were basically cheek to cheek as Seymour scrolled through. Again, I felt a swelling of pride as I looked at pictures that took us back through the many years Miss Liberty reigned in town. I was now a part of that, part of a tradition more sacred than anything else in this world.

"You posting this on *History Fits*?" Seymour asked Dulce.

Dulce nodded. "But Savvy thinks we need to do something bigger."

"We need to find a way to make everyone feel overwhelmed with memories at the same time," I said. "People gotta remember that this parade is the best thing that ever happened to Liberté."

Seymour gave Dulce back her phone and we returned to watching the documentary. Before long, Dulce was snoring. Seymour fell asleep a little later.

Per usual, I was wide-awake, anxiety making my brain hum. First, I wondered what Levi might do next. After that, I started wondering if Mom and Dad knew about the drama that was going on with Levi and her costumes. I doubted it. I certainly hadn't emailed them, and Glammy seemed to think that the less we bothered my parents, the sooner they would finish their business and come home.

I didn't like thinking about Mom and Dad. I was

homesick for them, even though I was the one who was still home, and that made zero sense. Emotions were weird that way.

Then I realized it wasn't just the homesickness that was making me sad; it was the fact that I was still awake. Being the last person to fall asleep at a sleepover is the loneliest feeling in the world.

I thought about the idea that Dulce and I had, the one about Miss Liberty's Greatest Hits. In fourth grade, we had taken a field trip to Philly to see a photography exhibit. A Miss Liberty museum exhibit would be way cool, but Liberté didn't have a museum. So what was left?

I'd told Dulce I'd think of something, but now I wasn't so sure.

18

The next morning was Monday. After Mrs. Bardot picked up Seymour and Dulce, I had my shift at Nifty Thrifty. It was totally boring. After stickering items with one-dollar and five-dollar labels, I headed to rehearsal, where life went from dull to frustrating.

I messed up two turning sequences, and everyone was off count for the middle ripple. At one point Bobbi twisted her necklace so hard that it broke. Pearls scattered everywhere, sounding like a hailstorm. We scrambled to gather them up for her, but to our shock, she just threw them in the trash.

"They're her fake ones," Tiara said, seeing our amazed looks.

"What's going on with your mom?" I asked softly.

"One, the Town Council refused to meet with her to discuss how to save the parade. Apparently they want to pour money into a new stadium for the high school. And two, Bobbi has no idea what your sister might do next."

"I don't either," I said. I knew I sounded defensive, but Levi was bringing out the defensiveness in me.

When I got home, I ran to the television. It was 5:20 p.m. At any minute Yvette would be giving the weather report, and all would be well. Until the next worry came along, at least.

But when I turned it on, it was Chad who was smiling at the camera. "To continue our special coverage of the stock market, we're going to be talking to financial expert Dominique Partello, who has worked at The New York City Stock Oversight Review since 2008. Dominique, can I ask—"

I turned it off. Financial news? Who cared about that?

I looked at my weather watch, but it didn't have the same soothing effect as a live weather report. So I just stared out the window. There was only blue sky: boring, flat, inactive blue sky.

"I'm heading out!" Levi startled me as she bounded downstairs. "Glammy's at dinner with her gal pals. Are you good for a while?"

"Where are you going?" *Invite me to come with you. Invite me to come with you.*

But she just picked up her book bag. "I need to get out of Liberté. The bus stops near the Caffeine Attack Coffee Shop in Whynot. It's got live music on Friday nights. Sorta punk meets indie rock."

I didn't know what that meant, but I nodded anyway.

"Okay. Why are you bringing your book bag if you're going to hear music?"

Levi flung open the front door. "I can listen to music and get work done. This Miss Liberty is nothing if not a multitasker."

Not long after Levi left, I called Seymour and Dulce for yet another sleepover. They were dropped off at eight.

"Levi will be gone for a few hours," I said, "and I want to check out her room. I think she's planning another rebellion. She said something about Miss Liberty multitasking. It gave me a bad feeling."

"So we're spying?" Dulce asked.

"I'm *preparing* for surprises," I retorted.

It was then that I saw that Seymour had a garment bag draped over his arm. "What's that?"

He held it high. "I like to think of this bag as the *chrysalis*—" he began, calling to mind our entomology lesson in science class this spring. "And this"—he unzipped the bag with a flourish—"is the *butterfly* ready to emerge from its cocoon."

The "butterfly" was a costume, a glorious costume

made from gold, bronze, and copper fabrics. The leotard was one-shouldered and the skirt a jagged cheerleader miniskirt made from gold, copper, and bronze panels.

"One shoulder?" Dulce breathed, pretending to fan herself. "How scandalous."

"It's not scandalous," Seymour insisted. "It's iconic. And it's an homage to Lady Liberty. See how the gold pleats at the torso, like her robes? Only, I thought gold would be better because—well, gold. I got the silhouette idea while watching *She-Ra* on Netflix, but then I saw images of female warriors like Athena and the Norse Valkyries in one of Dulce's books, and it got me thinking that Miss Liberty is a warrior version of Lady Liberty."

"It's beautiful," I said, wishing I had a stronger word than that.

"You made it so *shiny*," Dulce added, drawing a finger down a bronze panel.

Beneath her touch, the fabric resembled liquid gold, and I half believed that it could shift and shape itself to any dance movement.

"I was thinking—" Seymour began, heading to my room, where he gently laid the costume on the bed. "Savvy, maybe you could hold on to the costume and, when the time is right, show it to Levi. Maybe she can wear it after the show, you know, when the fireworks are going off. Or, if she's still doing the protest, she can wear it there. I just want my creation to be *seen*."

"I know the feeling." Then, realizing that time was wasting, I grabbed Dulce's and Seymour's wrists and pulled them into the hall. "Speaking of Levi, we need to go check out her room."

"What exactly are we looking for?" Dulce asked as they followed me back down the hall. "A diabolical plan in a journal that says 'diabolical plan'?"

I didn't say anything as I shoved open my sister's door, wincing as the hinge squeaked. Seymour and Dulce entered in front of me.

"Is her room different?" Seymour asked.

I froze and looked around. "Holy crud. She's redecorated." How did I not know that she had done this?

Gone were the dance posters and fairy lights. Her walls were now covered with posters of women working in science labs and winning gold medals. There was also something called the Youth Bill of Rights next to a quote by someone named Paulo Freire, a quote about dialogue and imposing structures, and I didn't totally understand it.

On the wall beside her vanity was a picture of Marlene Dietrich in a tux, as well as images of other women in tuxes. There was Rosie the Riveter and photos of people carrying signs about voting. One said *Ex-Felon Voting Bans Are Wrong* and another said *Support Your 18-year-old Who Wants to Vote*.

Seymour pointed at a photo of a girl who looked about Levi's age. A crown sat atop brown hair that fell straight down her back. She wore a white dress with sleeves that opened like a fan. She held up one hand and made a fist while the other hand held a bouquet of roses.

"Gotta be the 1970s," he said. "That long and straight hair is totally seventies."

Next to her photo was an article titled "Antiwar Miss Montana Takes a Stand, Gives Up a Crown."

"It says here," Seymour said, "that she was told that she couldn't keep being Miss Montana if she continued to discuss politics. She was against the Vietnam War. Rather than compromise, she gave up her title and was happy to do it."

"*Happy* to give up her crown?" I asked. "That's . . . I don't believe that. All right, let's just search. We're looking for . . . I don't know . . . to-do lists, or maybe photos." The truth was, I wasn't totally sure what we were looking for, only that I hoped I'd know it when I found it.

Next to Levi's clothes hamper was a pile of books with titles like *Best Speeches in U.S. History*; *Rebels with Causes*; and *Women Who Found Their Voices in the Twentieth Century*. I opened one, hoping Levi had highlighted or underlined something, but I didn't see any marks. Then I went through her drawers, tossing clothes on the ground. I didn't care if I was making a mess; I was on a mission. I just *had* to figure out what she was planning.

That's when I discovered a plastic bag stuffed in her sock drawer. Inside was a box of *hair dye*. Blue hair dye! The girl featured on the front of the box had "before" and "after" pictures. In the before picture, her hair was like mine—a total mud color—and after, it was the most beautiful shade of sapphire I'd ever seen.

"Look!" I shouted, holding it high. "Blue hair dye!"

"So?" Dulce asked, but Seymour's eyes were wide.

"Wow," he whispered. "Do you really think she's . . . I can't even say it."

"What?" Dulce pressed, looking between us. "What am I missing?"

"Bobbi is very strict about our appearances. It's not just the costumes she's rigid about, it's our total look," Seymour said. "We can't change anything right before a show. It's a *huge* no."

"This box means that Levi is planning on breaking that rule," I added. "It must be part of her next protest."

Dulce looked unconvinced. "What kind of protest requires hair dye?"

"I don't know. Everything she's doing is all for attention."

A thought occurred to me. If the dye was already gone, then Levi couldn't use it.

"Just throw it out," Dulce suggested.

"No," I said, reading the box. The directions seemed simple. I thought about how Levi was shocking everyone; how people couldn't help but talk about her, how lately she was even more impossible to overlook. Impossible to ignore—completely *seen*.

"I'm going to dye *my* hair."

"What?" Seymour gasped. "Why?"

"Be-*cause*, my sister thinks she's so rebellious, but let's see how she likes it when someone else is rebellious. When everyone is talking about me and not her, she'll finally know how it feels. Let's go."

Dyeing your hair is not what it looks like in the commercials. It's way harder.

Even though I was breaking the rules, I still felt a thrill shiver up my spine the second the liquid blue hit my scalp.

"I'm being rebellious," I sang to my reflection. "But in a good way."

"Mmm-hmm," Seymour hummed. He kept having to use his teeth to readjust the plastic gloves.

Dulce was sitting on the edge of the bathtub, watching us like we were conducting a science experiment and she was the judge.

"Rebellious in a good way?" she asked.

"Yep. I'm saying that I can seize the spotlight."

Seymour fumbled with the bottle, then dropped it. We all jumped back as the blue dye squirted across the floor.

"Whoops." He grimaced, picking up the bottle and looking inside. "Good news. Plenty left."

Dulce rolled her eyes. "This is getting messy. Savvy, where do you keep old towels? And cleaning supplies?"

"Above the washer," I said. Seymour set the bottle on

the counter. When he picked it up, a perfect blue ring was already staining the surface.

It felt like it took us hours, but at last we were done, and my hair was wrapped in a towel.

"How bright do you think it will be, Seymour?"

"*Bright*. I'm thinking neon peacock blue."

"Forget the color," Dulce said. "Let's just get this place cleaned up."

That's when we heard Levi's voice. "*Savvy!* What did you do to my room?!"

"Your sister's back already?" Seymour hissed.

Before I could answer, Levi was standing in the bathroom doorway, glaring at the three of us.

"You went through my drawers? You . . ." She paused and surveyed the bathroom. "Look at this mess! Is that my hair dye? Do you know how expensive that is?"

I grabbed the box and held it to my chest. "You were going to dye your hair for some stupid protest, so I beat you to it. You're not the only one who's rebellious . . . and . . . and—"

"I bought that hair dye because I'm teaching at a mermaid camp at the country club later this summer. I thought it would be fun to look the part."

My eyes widened. Dulce and Seymour were deadly quiet.

"What's with all the yelling?"

Oh great. Glammy was back too.

"Look at what she did, Glam. She trashed my room and *wasted* my hair dye, and just look at this bathroom!"

Glammy's jaw dropped when she stepped in the doorway. "What exactly is going on?"

"I thought I was being careful," Seymour said meekly.

"She ransacked my room!" Levi practically shrieked. "She *violated* my privacy!"

The way she said that made me feel like a slug.

"Savvy! Have you forgotten that we respect each other's space in this house?" Glammy said. "You shouldn't even be in your sister's room without permission, the same way she shouldn't be in yours. And, as for *this* disaster zone . . ." She shook her head, like she couldn't go on.

Levi shot me one last look of disgust before she stormed down the hall and into her room, slamming the door behind her.

"Well, I'm ready for bed," Dulce declared, exaggerating a yawn.

"Too bad," Glammy snipped. "You kids have lots of cleaning up to do."

19

It took us until three in the morning to get the dye off the walls and out from between every tile groove. When we were done, the bathroom reeked of nail polish remover (apparently an ideal cleaning agent) and Clorox. Before I went to bed, I stared at the mirror. I could see blue on my scalp, like someone had printed a line in cyan-blue ink from a printer. The rest of my hair was darker blue. Dragonfly-wing blue, telling me that I was becoming Levi-level cooler than cool.

The next morning—Tuesday—Glammy had to wake us up when Seymour's mom came to take Seymour and Dulce home. Before we said our groggy goodbyes, I pointed to my head, asking, "Well?"

Dulce leaned closer to examine me. "I'm not—it doesn't really look different."

"*Seriously?*" I asked, looking between her and Seymour.

Seymour pursed his lips, saying, "When we're out in the sun, I bet it will pop."

We heard a honk outside.

"Mom's antsy for some reason. See you later, Savvy," Seymour said.

"Bye."

When they were gone, I ran back to the bathroom, studying my hair. "I can't even see it," I grumbled.

It was then that Glammy popped in, coffee cup in hand. "Now that your friends are gone, we need to have a chat." She sat on the edge of the tub.

"Can we make this quick? You know lack of sleep can elevate my anxiety."

"I'm aware."

"*And* I have rehearsal this afternoon."

"I'm very, *very* aware. So tell me, what was last night all about?"

"I just . . . wanted to know what Levi was planning."

"So you decided to snoop in her room and make a mess. Then you jumped to conclusions when you saw that hair dye? Guess what you'll be doing *the rest* of the summer as punishment?"

"Working at Nifty Thrifty," I muttered.

"*Volunteering* at Nifty Thrifty," Glammy corrected. "And that will include cleaning the storage closet, mopping the floors, washing the windows—"

"Glammy, you don't get it. I did all that because I need this year to be perfect, and Levi keeps coming out with surprises that ruin everything. We need to do such a good job that people will remember how much they love the parade—"

"Honey, stop for a second and just listen. You can't control the future, and you can't control other people. The only thing you *can* do is enjoy this year's performance as much as possible. Worrying will rob you of every little moment. Don't let your anxieties make you miss the good stuff. Live in the now."

Didn't Glammy know how impossible that was for someone like me?

Rehearsals that afternoon started with Bobbi making an announcement. "I'm sure some of you have heard that we're having a projector in front of the stage this year. The mayor and I decided to get high-tech. We're going to create a backdrop that looks like it's constantly moving. While you all are dancing, images of flags are going to be rippling behind you. Any questions? . . . Yes, Mina?"

"Is it going to shine in our eyes?"

"No. The projector will be on a table in front of the stage, angled in such a way that you won't even notice it. Just a nice, patriotic backdrop that people will love. Now, places please."

The rest of rehearsal was brutal. I had never been told to work on my smile so much in my entire life.

"I want to be electrified!" Bobbi shouted. "Savvy, that smile is electrifying no one!"

To make things worse, no one noticed my hair. And I mean *no one*. People noticed everything about Levi: when she wore new earrings, when she looked tan, and when she went from spinning twenty-five times in a row to spinning twenty-seven times in a row. But no one noticed my hair.

To be fair, I was having a hard time seeing the blue, unless I got really close to the mirror. Maybe it was just as well. Maybe I wasn't ready to be a rebel.

Afterward, while Seymour and I packed up our stuff, Seymour got a text from Glammy.

Please tell Savvy that I called ahead for a bucket of chicken at Chicken Little. Pick up on the way home. Love you both.

Seymour chuckled. "I love how adults text so formally. I'll come with you; it's on my way."

The line at Chicken Little was almost out the door, but that was typical for five o'clock on a summer night.

"I don't like the smell in here," Seymour whispered, wrinkling his nose.

"Ssh," I hissed, looking around. I didn't want anyone overhearing us, thinking that we were disrespecting a favorite fast-food dinner choice. I had enough problems with my sister sabotaging the parade.

"Hey, Seymour. Picking up dinner?" It was Seymour's

neighbor, Mrs. Clements. She had two plastic bags in her hands; I could smell the buttermilk fried chicken.

"No. I'm just here with Savvy."

The second Seymour said my name, Mrs. Clements's expression changed from friendly to icy. "Well, at least the Montrose family is supporting *something* in this town."

I flinched.

"Rude," Seymour muttered as she walked away.

"Hey. Hey—Savvy."

Seymour and I turned around. I didn't recognize the man talking to me. He was wearing a shirt that said *If you think man evolved from apes, I got a book for you.*

"Yes?" Seymour asked for me, ever polite.

"I don't appreciate your sister disrespecting our town."

Never in the history of my face getting hot had it gotten this hot. Other people were starting to look at us. "I don't know what you're talking about," I said quietly.

"Oh, I think you know exactly what I'm talking about."

Every conversation stopped; even the fryers in the back seemed to sizzle at a lower volume.

"Gene, just ignore them," a woman said.

"I don't think I can. This girl's sister is making a mockery of our parade. *Our* traditions."

"Oh?" Seymour asked. "*Your* traditions? You used to dance in the parade?"

"Excuse me?" Gene demanded.

Seymour pulled out his pearly white fan, snapped it

open, and started waving it in front of his face. "I *think* you heard me."

A few people in line actually gasped. My mouth, meanwhile, was dry; my brain was spinning. Bert started dancing in my head.

"Listen, you little—"

"My sister isn't making a mockery of anything," I interrupted. "This is her third year as Miss Liberty, and she takes it very seriously."

"She's mocking the title and its history," another woman snorted.

"Exactly, Jenni. Thank you!" Gene nodded. "First a tuxedo, and then the other costume."

"*Look*, my sister is trying to say something important about the fact that the voting place has been moved to . . . somewhere else."

Wait—why am I defending Levi?

"It's not her job to say anything," Jenni said. "That's the point of Miss Liberty. She dances, she smiles. The end."

"If your sister can't do as she's told, she should be removed," Gene said. "End of story."

Do as she's told? I looked at Seymour. His eyes were as big as mine felt.

"My sister isn't doing anything wrong. You're just . . . I don't know . . . uncomfortable that she is talking about voting. It's just voting. I mean, *you* vote, right?"

"Of course I vote!" Gene snapped.

"We all do," Jenni agreed. "You know, mostly in the big, important elections."

Big, important elections? Did that mean there were times when voting wasn't big or important?

Jenni just kept talking. "It's not like she has a difficult job; the girl just has to perform. We don't need to hear her voice."

Gene snorted. "We don't *want* to hear her voice."

Tears sprang to my eyes. The way he spoke was so . . . I don't know. Cruel. Dismissive. Like not only were my sister's words not important, but my *sister* wasn't important.

"We're going," I hissed, grabbing Seymour's arm.

"But the chicken?"

"We'll have peanut butter and jelly," I snapped.

"Where's the chicken?"

I barely heard Glammy as I headed for Levi's room. Levi was lying on her stomach on her bed, reading. Instead of reminding me to knock, she actually smiled when I burst in.

"Hey, destructo-girl. I've decided to get over the fact that you stole my dye and trashed my room. Glammy reminded me that we're all stressed right now, so I'm electing to chill."

For a second, I just stared at her. Levi and I never physically fought. We might have yelled and slapped each other playfully, but that was nothing like what I wanted to do now. I wanted to pull her hair or shove her off the bed. She was acting mellow, and here I had just been yelled at trying to buy dinner. So I walked over to her desk and swept my arm across the top, sending her pencils and mini stapler flying.

"Hey!" Levi shouted.

"You're making my anxiety worse!"

"So your solution is to make another mess?! I've got news for you, Savvy—something those anxiety exorcism books don't tell you. No one can make your anxiety worse but yourself."

"That's not true. Circumstances—"

"Savvy, listen to me. Get a grip. Stop absorbing everyone else's feelings and opinions. No one can make you feel what you don't want to feel. No one can make you feel stressed or important or anxious but yourself."

"Levi, you're making everyone look at me like I'm disrespecting the Miss Liberty title, too, *which I'm so not*. Really, *you're* the drama. You should have heard everyone at the chicken place. I was trying to pick up dinner, and they all started attacking me. And—"

"Wait. Stop. People attacked you? Who? Give me names."

I hesitated. "They didn't *attack* me. But they were glaring and yelling and looming—"

"Looming?"

"Yeah. Like this." I puffed up my chest and leaned

forward, curling my shoulders so that I loomed like a bodybuilder.

Levi was fighting a smile. I could tell.

"This isn't funny."

"I'm sorry. Tell me exactly what people were doing. And saying."

"They asked me why you were disrespecting the Miss Liberty title. I tried to remember what you've been saying about voting and the voting location, but I couldn't recall your exact words."

She frowned. "You don't need my exact words, Savvy. You need to have your own words."

A growl scraped the back of my throat. "I *have* my own words, and I have my own goals, and you're getting in the way of them. In fact, I have my entire life mapped out, and it's a perfect trajectory, except you're ruining it because you're being selfish. You've been Miss Liberty for so long that it's not shiny and special for you anymore."

I took a deep breath, trying to make my heart slow down. It felt like someone was doing a drum solo in my chest. Levi was ruining my plans. It wasn't just about being Miss Liberty. It was about knowing what I was doing from Sunday to Sunday and then starting all over again on Monday.

"You know what?" Levi said. "I don't think you're upset with me. You're upset, but not with me."

"You're making me feel like I'm losing my mind!" I snapped before storming out of Levi's room.

Her voice followed me. "And no one can make you feel that way but yourself."

She sounded almost happy, like she'd figured something out that had been bothering her for years.

20

That night, a miracle happened: I fell asleep with no problem. Maybe all the worrying had a plus side; it had exhausted Bert.

I woke up when I heard someone whispering my name. Opening my eyes, I saw Levi standing over me, fully dressed.

"What's wrong?" I asked. "Is it Glammy?"

"She's fine. We're going on a road trip. You and me."

I looked at the clock. It was three in the morning. "Road trip?"

"A baby road trip. Get dressed."

We took the Kronk, Glammy's Jeep Cherokee circa 1991 that made creaking and knocking sounds every time it was put into drive. Noises aside, it was pretty reliable.

"Okay," Levi said, starting the engine. "I'm going to put the odometer on zero so we can clock how far we're about to drive. Ready?" The Kronk groaned as she shifted into drive.

We drove and drove.

"Seriously, where are we going?"

"To a land of once upon a time and far, far away," Levi said dreamily.

I shot her a look. She just laughed. "We're going approximately forty minutes outside of town."

I watched Liberté disappear in the rearview mirror and then stared straight ahead at the open road. It was as wide as an airport runway.

"There's nothing out here," I said.

Levi nodded. "Kinda desolate."

We passed three Miss Liberty billboards, all with Levi's face. They were positioned one right after the other so that the sentence from the first billboard carried to the second, and that one carried to the third.

The first said: *Are you ready?*

The second: *For this year's . . .*

The third billboard finished the question: *Miss Liberty Fourth of July Parade?*

"Isn't it exciting to see your face up there?" I asked.

Levi leaned forward. "I'm pretty numb to it, to be honest."

Not knowing how to respond, I went back to focusing

on the heavens. The bowl of the sky was so dark, I wondered if the stars had gotten lost. But even as I tried to find constellations, I couldn't get the confrontation at the restaurant out of my head. Whenever something embarrassing happens, I tend to relive it over and over again. I hate that about myself.

"There are so many things I want to say," Levi whispered. I couldn't tell if she was talking to me or to herself. "For the first time in my life, I don't even want to dance. I want to talk. And be loud."

"So talk. Just don't stop doing what's important for the parade."

"I don't even know if I know how to say what I want to say. It's like when you're getting a fountain drink and you stop paying attention, and suddenly the soda overflows and it's all over the floor before you notice."

I laughed. "Your words are soda."

Levi giggled too. "Yep, spilling everywhere, making a mess."

"What flavor would you be if you were a soda?"

"Oh, wow. Okay, um, anything with cherry."

I should have known that. I've seen Levi eat a whole jar of maraschino cherries in one sitting. "I'd be root beer."

"Ew. Savvy, root beer makes you burp."

"I know. That's why I like it. All my anxiety gets out in a couple of big burps."

That had us both cracking up.

We passed our third firecracker stand. *Get your Miss Liberty Fireworks Here!*

"You know," Levi began, "people say that Miss Liberty stands for America and freedom and, well, liberty, obviously. But they don't seem bothered that she doesn't *do* anything. She's so quiet."

"You want to be loud?" I asked.

"It'd be nice."

Giggling, I rolled down my window, leaned out, and started howling.

"Savvy!"

"Try it."

She looked at me like I was the biggest daredevil she'd ever met.

"Try it, Levi. Come on."

She rolled her eyes. "Fine." Rolling her window down, she started yelling too.

That's how we drove for at least a mile, howling into the darkness as loud as we could.

Finally, we eased into a gravel parking lot outside an abandoned white building. The clock in the car read 4:25 a.m.

"The odometer is at forty-eight miles," Levi said. "That's how far out of town we are. It will take anyone forty-five minutes to an hour to get here, depending on traffic."

"Where is 'here'?"

"This is where people have to drive in order to vote.

They used to vote at the old post office, and now they have to come all the way out here."

"Oh. *Oh*."

"Yep."

"But you don't vote."

"Savvy, I turn eighteen in five weeks. I get to vote this year. And it's a big deal. It's what we've been talking about nonstop in civics class. Not to mention I've been looking forward to it since forever. Remember when we were little and we'd get to accompany Glammy when she went to vote?"

Before moving in with us, Glammy used to come over early on voting days. She'd make pancakes in the shape of flags, with red, white, and blue icing on top. Then she'd tell us about how when she was young, women couldn't have credit cards in their own name, that it took marches and protests to change that.

"And this place isn't just for Liberté," Levi continued. "It's also for Whynot, Alston, Paris, and Liontown. One voting location for five towns, because their locations have also closed. Five times the traffic to this one place. Do you know how people get their rights stepped on? Gradually. Does that building look like it can handle five times the normal traffic?"

I wasn't sure what the normal amount of traffic was, let alone what five times that phantom number looked like. But I could tell that my sister wanted me to agree with her, so I just said, "No. It does not."

"No, it does not," Levi echoed.

We sat there for a moment.

"Dulce's family doesn't have a car," I said.

"And now they'll have to figure out the logistics on voting day. Other families too. What if someone can't get off work, or they need a babysitter? And people have jobs that don't always let them take time off. Voting should be a federal holiday, but that's my next fight. And people don't always have reliable cars. There's no bus stop near here. There's that gas station across the way and a few firecracker stands. So you know what might happen?"

I honestly didn't.

"People won't vote. They'll want to, but it will be too hard, too inconvenient. And, if Miss Liberty can't say something, then I don't know what I'm doing in her costume."

Levi put the Kronk in reverse, and we slowly rolled away from what might have been the emptiest building in the whole wide world.

21

We pulled into our driveway at 6:39 a.m. Since we had been up all night, I felt like we were watching the Wednesday morning sunrise from the wrong angle.

Then something strange caught my eye. There was a bunch of trash on our lawn.

Levi turned off the Kronk. For a minute, we both just stared. Then our front door opened and Glammy charged out. "Seriously? You girls go out in the middle of the night and don't even leave a note..."

Her voice trailed off as she saw the garbage: disposable coffee cups, napkins, and straw wrappers from McDonalds, empty makeup vials, rotten lettuce heads, lidless detergent bottles, and shredded pieces of paper blowing around like confetti.

"Holy hairspray and hairdos!" Glammy cried.

Levi and I climbed out of the Kronk. "Remember that time Dad said we should get a security system with cameras, and we all laughed?" Levi asked dryly.

"Are you smiling?" I demanded.

"I'm sorry," Levi said, clearly trying to hide her smile. "I'm tired. Ignore me."

"Hey guys, what's . . . going on . . ."

I turned around. Stevie and her mom were driving past our house, and both leaned out of the driver's window of the car.

"Oh, hey, Willa!" Glammy called. I could tell she was wishing that they hadn't driven by at that exact moment. "What are you two doing up so early?"

"Meeting Mina and her mom for doughnuts and coffee. Did someone dump this in your yard?"

A few hamburger wrappers stuck to my ankles. I swatted at them, but the melted cheese acted like sticky tape.

"I guess it's someone's idea of a joke," Glammy growled.

"What's that?" Stevie asked, pointing at our mailbox. Taped to the front was a piece of white paper. Written on it in bright red letters were the words Trash for a Trashy Miss Liberty.

For a second, no one said anything. It was almost as if the words were written in neon lights that were lasering our eyes.

"That's so mean," Stevie said, sounding like she meant it.

"It is a bit . . . harsh," Levi agreed. She wasn't smiling or laughing anymore.

"Bobbi, you are not going to believe this," Stevie's mom was saying, speaking into her phone. I saw Stevie avoid my eyes as she settled back in her seat.

"Trashy Miss Liberty, my royal a—" Glammy stopped herself. She grabbed Levi's face, holding her cheeks. "Anyone who would do this is trashy. You hear me? *They* are the trashy ones."

Levi nodded. Stevie and her mom rolled away slowly, like they needed to take a long, lingering look at our mess. Had Stevie looked away because she felt guilty? Had Tiara and Stevie and Mina done this?

No. No way. Or . . .

Levi just stared after them, as if she were about to cry. If someone had called me trashy, I would absolutely be crying, but Levi wasn't a crier.

"Maybe I should call your parents. Tell them to come home."

"No," Levi said. Even though her voice was shaky, she sounded firm. "They're doing something important, and *I'm* doing something important, and I think . . . I think we have to see everything through."

Levi squeezed Glammy's hand, wiped the tear that I wasn't even sure was there, and went back into the house, leaving the trash behind her.

Rehearsal that afternoon was a "marking" rehearsal. Marking rehearsals are when you just walk through the dance on the real stage, making sure you know where to go. Bobbi believed that marking rehearsals helped dress rehearsals run more smoothly. Today, that meant roasting in the hot sun. (Eighty-eight degrees, according to my watch, with no hope of clouds.)

As we walked from one formation to the other, Bobbi took her time straightening the lines. When she was on the other side of the stage, I leaned toward Seymour. "Can you see the blue in my hair *now*?"

He squinted. "Not really. Maybe we didn't leave it in long enough. I mean, your roots look darker."

"Savvy, Seymour, no chitchatting!" Bobbi shouted from the front of the stage. "Savvy, you're supposed to be at the front right corner."

"Sorry." I hurried to the corner where Stevie and Tiara stood, loving the slapping-smacking sounds my character shoes made on the stage.

I found my spot, then shielded my eyes from the sun as I faced the street. Dulce was out there, her clipboard at her feet as she took photos.

I waved, and she waved back. Then Bobbi was suddenly in front of me, blocking my view and the sun.

"*Where* is Levi?"

"Not sure. She said she'd meet me here."

"Clearly, she's *not* here. Which means she's skipping. Since when does your sister skip?"

I shook my head. Everyone was staring at me, but I had no words. Skipping dance classes or practice for anything other than extreme sickness was a sin in our dance world.

"Bobbi," Tiara scoffed, wiping sweat from her brow. "Why do you even need Levi? This is her third year doing this dance. She doesn't need to mark her spot."

Hands on her hips, Bobbi inhaled and exhaled. Her nostrils flared like Calypso, an iguana Seymour used to have. "It's a good thing she opted *not* to go on our New York City trip tomorrow. I wouldn't let her go even if she begged me."

22

The next day, the first thing Seymour did when we got on the bus bound for New York City was show me Dulce's latest article.

Right away I saw the words "Greatest Hits" at the top and gave a happy little squeal of recognition.

THE GREATEST HITS OF THE MINISKIRT

Fashion protests are usually about more than fashion. Just look at the miniskirt. More specifically, look at the miniskirt protest that started in England. In the 1960s, the miniskirt was a sign of feminism and liberation. In 1966, when the haute couture designer (*haute couture* means high fashion, my dear readers) Christian Dior did not feature miniskirts in their fashion show, a group of women known as the British Society for the Protection of Mini Skirts marched outside the venue, demanding to be seen and heard. That brings us to this article's big question: How important is clothing when it comes to being heard? This was most definitely one of the defining moments, or "greatest hits" of the miniskirt. There's been a lot of debate in town about costumes, but when is the costume more important than the person wearing it?

"Look," Seymour said. "She even made a miniskirt slideshow."

I pulled my knees to my chest as Seymour tapped the screen. Slides played the same way they did at school presentations, but this one showed models from different decades, all wearing miniskirts.

"That's Twiggy," Seymour said, pointing to a blonde with eyes as big as binocular lenses. "She was—"

He paused because Tiara had chosen that moment to suddenly pop up in front of us and lean over the bus seat. "So your sister really isn't coming?"

"No," I said. I didn't want to start the day focusing on my sister and her drama.

Tiara sniffed. "Like Bobbi said, it's probably for the best."

"Wait—are we talking about Levi?" Mina asked. She and Stevie were sitting in their own seat across the aisle, leaving Tiara to lounge all by herself. "I heard *all* about the trash dumped in your yard, Savvy. Did it make Levi realize she should maybe just quit? My mom said that it probably would."

"Well, tell your mom that it didn't and it won't!" I snapped.

Mina wasn't done. "Your sister is being totally disrespectful to the entire Miss Liberty brand—"

"We're a *brand*?" Seymour snickered.

Tiara drummed her fingers on our seat. "Mina is right. With all those cameras—"

"Look! New York City!" Stevie shouted, pointing out the window.

Saved by the New York City skyline.

I've never told anyone this, but cities intimidate the heck out of me. It sounds silly to be intimidated by buildings, but it's true. My brain tightens at the thought of all those things packed and stacked on top of one another. I always felt as though cities wanted to eat me up, devour me. I want to hurry back home but also stay right where I am.

As everyone oohed and aahed and said, "We're here!" all I could think was, *Why can't I be excited? Why do I have to worry all the time?*

Seymour caught my eye; I forced a grin. It was too late to hide my anxiety, but I could at least hide my fear underneath a smile.

After all, it's what a future Miss Liberty would do.

✦ ✦ ✦

No two dance studios categorize beginner, intermediate, and advanced classes the same way, so when you take a class outside your own studio, the levels can feel strange. Maybe your studio has an advanced class that is considered beginner somewhere else.

Still, when you only have one day at a studio, you always stick with your group, and Bobbi had signed us all up for an intermediate jazz class. About twenty seconds into it, I realized that at the New York Lights Dance Studio, I wasn't intermediate; I was a beginner.

The teacher's name was Iona, and she had more excitement in her pinkie than any one of us had in our entire bodies. She had us line up in the back. The class consisted of all kinds of dancers; I could tell who was a professional and who wasn't. Professional dancers have a stance. Not just a look, but a no-nonsense, I'll-never-flinch stance.

I didn't have that stance.

Tiara was on my left, with Stevie and Mina on her left. They were wearing ripped black tights over their leotards.

"Your tights are ripped," I whispered.

Tiara just gave me a look. "That's what *real* dancers wear."

All right!" Iona called, clapping her hands. "I got some new faces in here. You all from out of town?"

Tiara rolled her shoulders back and smiled. But before she could open her mouth, I jumped in. "Yes we are!"

Everyone looked at me. I just rolled my shoulders back,

popped my right foot, and put my hands on my hips. "We're from Liberté. It's home to the Miss Liberty parade."

Iona gave me the biggest smile. "That is just fabulous! I've heard of that parade. Are you here to get your rhythm on?"

I nodded.

Iona winked at me. "I'm loving the enthusiasm! Let's all try to channel that and make this a killer class! Face the front—and five, six, seven, eight—"

I was on fire during warm-ups, able to anticipate Iona's every move. Once we were done warming up, Iona said, "Okay, my lovelies, I'm going to be honest: I threw this together this morning. I had another number planned, but it just didn't feel right, so I thought, what the heck? We're performers. We're at our best when we're spontaneous."

It felt like she was looking right at me when she said that.

The routine started with a strut, and then it got super complicated, with turns and kicks. Iona broke us up into groups. When it was my group's turn, I was fine . . . at first. But then the music sped up and I totally forgot the steps. For a second I froze in the middle of the floor while everyone danced around me. In the mirror, I looked ridiculous. I couldn't just stand there; I had to do something!

As my panic built, my feet started to itch, the muscles beginning to spasm. I realized that my feet needed to stamp. And scuff. And pound the ground. Following my instincts, I started tapping. It didn't matter that I was wearing jazz shoes, I still tapped and tapped, creating a rainstorm of sound.

The balls of my feet stung; that's how hard I was hitting the floor. For a second, maybe two, all my worries were dandelion fuzz shrinking in the studio's air-conditioning. Miss Liberty and her drama didn't even exist. Nothing existed but my improvisation. Then I realized that everyone was staring at me, and I stopped.

"*Wow*!" Iona cried, clapping like she wanted an encore. "That's called improvising your heart out!"

I could barely breathe. My legs were tingling, and I felt sweaty and wonderful. "I forgot the steps, so I just listened to my body and—"

"Followed the music! I got ya." Iona faced the other dancers. "We all know the most sacred rule of dance. If we forget the choreography, what do we do?"

Silence, then Tiara cleared her throat. "We keep on dancing."

"That's *right*! And if we're getting tired, what do we do?"

This time Tiara, Mina, and Stevie said the words together: "Keep on *dancing*!"

"And when we're feeling scared, what do we do?"

This time the rest of us joined in: *"Keep. On. Dancing!"*

"No matter what," Iona finished. "No matter what, we keep on dancing." This time she winked, and I could have sworn the wink was just for me.

✦ ✦ ✦

Contact was the most amazing musical I've ever seen. The story was told entirely through dance. There were three sections, and each took place in a different time period, but I will always and forever remember Act III. In that act, there was a woman in a yellow dress. Everyone else was in drab colors, so she didn't fit in at all, but she didn't care. In a dress as yellow as a taxicab, she walked and strutted until it was time to dance. One of the songs she danced to was one of my dad's favorites—"Simply Irresistible" by Robert Palmer—and that was followed by "Sing, Sing, Sing."

"That's one of our songs," Seymour whispered triumphantly. We watched that yellow skirt twirl and ripple like an umbrella in one of Glammy's cocktails. "It's weird," he mused.

"What?"

"Sometimes I forget that dance is supposed to be fun."

The girl in yellow was spinning, having the time of her life. I knew that feeling. I had felt it today in class, and not because I had performed a choreographed routine perfectly but because I had danced the way I'd wanted to, letting my feet tell me what to do.

After the performance, we all gathered in the lobby.

"I'm going to do something a bit unprecedented," Bobbi announced.

None of the other dancers seemed to hear my aunt; even

girls like Ellie, Mazie, and Paloma—normally considered to be the "quiet" ballerinas—were bubbling with excitement.

"Did you see her spins?" Ellie gasped.

"Did you hear our song?" her sister Mazie asked.

"Seymour, do you think you could twirl me like that?" Paloma asked.

"Ahem." Bobbi cleared her throat as loud as she could.

We faced her dutifully.

"As I was saying, I'm going to do something unprecedented: give you all precisely one hour to wander around this theater. There are not one but two gift shops right here in the theater. You just walk under that archway there. But remember, it's only for an hour, and then we all have to meet back here so we can get on the bus and head home. All right?"

We nodded.

As everyone started to disperse, Seymour grabbed my hand. "Fashion Mart," he whispered. "It's across the street, and it'll take a half hour, tops. *Please.* I drool over the costumes online. I want to see them in person."

I looked for Bobbi and saw that she was already in the gift shop, not paying attention to us.

"Fine." I sighed. "Let's go."

We ducked out the theater's front doors and ran across the street. When we walked through the door of Fashion Mart, Seymour sighed. "My happy place."

I don't know how much time we spent looking at the clothes, which ranged from the tailored to the fantastical.

"Look at these," I said, holding up two fans made from scarlet feathers. "Seymour, these are totally you."

"Those were used in *My Fair Lady*," the clerk called out. He was sitting at a desk, surrounded by bobbleheads of Dorothy Gale, Dolly Parton, and Godzilla. He didn't look that much older than Levi. I wondered if he was in college.

"Really?" Seymour breathed. "That makes it even better. How much? I don't see a price tag."

The clerk cocked his head. "I believe they're thirty a piece, but you seem like you'll appreciate such a purchase, so how about fifteen?"

"Done!" Seymour called, digging in his pocket.

While Seymour paid for the fans, the clerk asked, "You kids from out of town?"

Seymour nodded. "We came to see *Contact*."

"Such a fantastic revival!" the clerk declared. "The way the dancer in yellow *owns* the stage."

"I have been looking for you children everywhere!"

We all jumped. Bobbi was standing in the store's foyer, flanked by Tiara, Stevie, and Mina.

"I told you they snuck out, Bobbi!" Mina snapped, putting one hand on her hip.

Bobbi just glared at us, her eyes fluttering over Seymour before landing on me. "I thought I'd made it clear that—"

She suddenly made a choking sound, and her mouth

literally froze. She was gaping at something behind us, her eyes as round as saucers.

"Mom?" Tiara asked. Then she looked behind our heads. "Oh. *Oh!*"

"Is that . . ." Mina began.

"It is," Stevie finished.

Slowly, I turned around. I couldn't *believe* I hadn't seen it before. There, in the middle of the store, on a lanky mannequin painted orange, was the Miss Liberty costume. *Our* Miss Liberty costume. In front of her plastic toes was an easel with a card that read "Miss Liberty costume from America's longest-running Fourth of July Parade. *Donation courtesy of the town of Liberté.*"

23

The bus ride home was quiet. About forty-five minutes in, Bobbi slid into my seat. Her skin looked almost splotchy, like she was having an allergic reaction. Her pearls were balled up in her fist at her throat. I recognized them as her backup pearls, because their color was off-white, the shade of vanilla ice cream. According to Tiara, Bobbi had an entire jewelry box full of extra pearl necklaces.

She didn't say anything at first. When she finally spoke, her voice was flat and husky. "Levi *donated* our costume. She *gave* it away."

I said nothing. What *could* I say?

"A costume that's been in use since the 1950s!"

"I'm so sorry—" I began, even though I hated apologizing for stuff that wasn't my fault.

"I'm trying so hard," Bobbi whispered, staring straight ahead, "*so hard* to ensure that our parade goes off without a hitch, so everyone will remember how important it is."

She made a choking sound again. Oh my gosh. Was Bobbi about to *cry*? I didn't know she *could* cry.

But she didn't. Instead, she pressed her fingers to her temples. "I just want the parade to stay as it is. I want our summers to stay as they are."

"Me too."

Bobbi slumped in her seat. At first I was worried that she'd had a stroke, or an aneurysm or something serious, because Bobbi never slumped. *Never.* Sitting or standing, her posture was perfect.

I wanted to help. Should I tell her about the "greatest hits"? No, Bobbi wouldn't love anything that wasn't her idea. What else could I do?

"Never mind." Bobbi sat up, patting her cheeks. "It'll all work out. It has to. I still have my luncheon to remind everyone that our parade is central to Liberté's identity, that its positive, no-questions-asked embrace of patriotism is something we can count on. At my luncheon, I *will* convince everyone that the parade is too important to let go."

When she rose to return to the front of the bus, I could have sworn she was patting her cheeks to keep tears from ruining her mascara.

✦ ✦ ✦

"Savvy, Savvy, you need to look at this."

Somewhere in New Jersey, I had fallen asleep. When I opened my eyes, Seymour had his phone turned toward me so I could see the screen. The image was of my sister. When I saw what she was doing, my body went cold.

"Is she . . . ?"

"Burning the American flag?" Seymour murmured, snapping open his fan, hiding us behind its red lace. "Um, yeah."

There was Levi, sitting on a curb of a sidewalk, wearing opaque sunglasses, looking chill as she sat next to an American flag that was bunched up like a used tissue and in flames.

My stomach heaved. *Am I going to throw up? No, no, I can't throw up in front of people.* That was one of my worst fears: puking in front of a crowd. Where was the bathroom? All the way in the back of the bus. Crud!

I looked at the photo again. The more I studied it, the more confused I felt. Flags weren't just a symbol of America; they were a symbol of Miss Liberty. Her costume was based on its colors, for crying out loud.

"But here's the thing," Seymour began. "If you ask me, something looks off with this photo." Then he frowned. "Wait, where did my signal go?" He began to shake his phone, as if that would help. "We must be in a dead zone or—are we slowing down?"

A few seconds later, in the middle of nowhere, our bus rolled to a stop.

✦ ✦ ✦

Bobbi and the driver seemed to argue for hours.

"What do you mean the gas sensor is on?" Bobbi demanded. "I don't even know what that means. And why would the bus just stop because of a sensor?"

"Ma'am," the driver began, "it's like I've been saying. The system is trying to tell me that we don't have gas, but that's not possible. I just filled up. Give me a second." He hopped off the bus to investigate.

"For those of you who have cell phones, are any of them getting service?" Bobbi called, holding up her phone.

Every dancer with a phone started waving it back and forth, searching for a signal. I craned my neck out the window to see where we were. That's when I saw Levi's billboard, the one that had finished the question with: *Miss Liberty Fourth of July Parade?*

"I know where we are," I declared, poking Seymour. But he was messing with his phone and tuning me out.

Looking back at the billboard, I had a blinding burst of energy, a sense of purpose. The idea of sitting on this bus while everyone fiddled with their phones seemed inconceivable. I needed to *do* something—get up and fix the fact that we were stranded.

Still stabbing her phone, Bobbi paced the length of the aisle. I waited until she reached the back of the bus before I eased out of my seat.

"I know where there's a gas station," I whispered to Seymour. "I'm going to go get help. Tell Bobbi I'll be right back."

He didn't really hear me until I reached the front of the bus. "Wait," Seymour said. "Savvy, what'd you say?"

"Savvy?" I heard Bobbi call a moment later, but I was already down the steps and out the door.

"I'll be right back!" I hollered over my shoulder.

And I was off. Behind me, I could hear my aunt shout, "No! Savvy! What are you—SAV-VY! Gosh darn—"

And I ran. Simple as that.

If I remembered correctly, it had taken roughly five minutes by car to reach the new voting location from that last billboard. I remember because I had checked my weather watch and the Kronk's clock when we passed it the first time. And I had checked both again when we pulled into the parking lot.

If it had taken five minutes by car, it would take maybe seven or eight minutes on foot, right? Then I'd be at the gas station, and I could call for help, and everyone would be thrilled at my quick thinking in a crisis. Talk about a Liberty Line dancer taking action!

I looked at my weather watch: Seventy-seven degrees. Low humidity. Eight fifty-five p.m.

I was on my own. I waited to feel panic, but it didn't come. Instead I almost felt tipsy on freedom. I didn't even know where Bert was. Had he vanished? For the first time, I wasn't worried about him.

This had to be a good thing, right?

✦ ✦ ✦

Fifteen minutes later, I was still walking.

Twenty-five minutes later and I was *still* walking.

So far, only two cars had passed me, and neither had slowed down. Not that I wanted them to.

Twilight colors soaked the sky, lavenders and navy blues and dusky pinks all swirling around a moon that was just starting to rise, oval and tilted over the horizon.

The sky was still light enough that I could see the ribbon of road stretch before me. It didn't take me long to decide that roads are different, longer and wider, when you're walking versus when you're in a car.

I knew my aunt hadn't followed me, she had a busload full of kids to watch, but where was Seymour? Wouldn't he have followed me?

Keep walking, Savvy. Get to the gas station and save the day. Manifest positivity. Manifest positivity.

There it was! The brightly lit station on one side of the road, the new voting location on the other. The voting building looked smaller than it had when I was here with Levi. No wonder she was so determined to keep voting in town. This new headquarters might as well have been in another state. I was finally starting to understand her frustration. The question was—

HONK! HONK!

I jumped a mile and fell back onto the shoulder. The bus barreled toward me, brakes squealing as it screeched to a stop right next to me.

The door flung open. Bobbi stood on the middle step,

her eyes wider than I had ever seen them. "Savvy, get on this bus this instant before I *blister your butt*! Now!"

Without a word, I rushed onto the bus.

It was close to midnight by the time we pulled up to the dance studio. Looking at my weather watch, I saw the word "Friday" just below an emoji of a moon with a sleepy smile.

Several times during the ride, Bobbi had walked over to my seat like she was about to say something, but then she pursed her lips, shook her head, and stormed away.

"I've never seen her so angry," Tiara whispered.

Seymour just scolded me. "I can't believe you ran off like that. You could have been kidnapped! Or hit by a car!"

I sank lower in my seat. "How did you all fix the bus?"

"The gas cap had been screwed on at an angle," Seymour explained. "It made the bus think that the tank was empty."

Parents were already waiting at the studio, ready to pick us up. But so were reporters and photographers. There were flashes as soon as the bus doors opened.

"Hello, paparazzi," Mina hummed, sounding almost gleeful.

"They're probably here because of Levi," Stevie observed. "Hard to forget a picture of Miss Liberty next to a burning flag."

We filed off the bus, Bobbi standing in front to shield us from the crowd.

"We had a minor gas cap and sensor issue on the road," Bobbi said, using her pleasant hostess voice. "Of course, I understand you have questions about Miss Liberty. Rest assured that changes are on the way. But if you'll excuse me for a moment . . ."

Cutting in front of us, she power walked over to Glammy, who was sitting in the Kronk.

"I'm in so much trouble," I said for the umpteenth time.

"Well, you should be!" Seymour said, snapping open his Fashion Mart fan. "You scared me to death. There are kidnappers everywhere, you know."

Glammy's eyes got big, and I saw her lips form my name. Then she shook her head and said something I couldn't hear. Bobbi nodded and stepped to the side. Their eyes landed on me at the same time. Bobbi stormed past me, returning to talk to the reporters. As she did, her facial expression changed from fury to charm in about 2.5 seconds.

"Savvy, get in the car now!" Glammy bellowed. "Seymour, you too! I already told your mom you'd be sleeping at our house."

Glammy glared at me in the rearview mirror as soon as I got into the back seat. "Bobbi filled me in on your little stunt," she growled, putting the car in drive. "Holy hairspray and hairdos, did you really go running down the interstate in the middle of the night?"

"I was being proactive."

"Proactive? Try stupid and dangerous and . . . and . . . *stupid*. Do you have any idea what could have happened to you? You could have been kidnapped—"

"That's what I said," Seymour cut in.

"Or hit by someone speeding, or a million other things. And how dare you leave Bobbi like that. How was she supposed to run after you?"

"She wasn't. I was just—"

"I wasn't asking for an excuse. She had a bus full of dancers, and out of all of them, you are one of the responsible ones. Or so we thought." Glammy shook her head a few more times, glaring at me in the rearview mirror. "Not okay, Savvy. And the only reason I'm not making you hitchhike home is because we have another family crisis waiting for us."

24

"That's not me."

Levi said those words matter-of-factly, like she was ordering a soda. She had been waiting for us at the kitchen table when we got home. Now we were all sitting around like we were about to have a séance or play Go Fish. I think a séance might have been more useful.

"The costume at Fashion Mart or the flag burning?" I asked.

Glammy snapped her fingers at me. "Excuse me, but you don't get to sound judgmental, Miss Run Down the Highway Like a Lunatic."

Levi looked from Glammy to me and back again. "Okay, I'm not even asking what that is all about. And yes, I did donate the Miss Liberty costume. But that photo of me and the burning flag? No way. I wouldn't do that."

"Why not?" I demanded.

"Because I'm trying to get people to pay attention to the way we vote locally. That has nothing to do with burning a flag; there's no symbolism there for me. Also, I've put *thought* into what I'm doing. I chose the tux because I wanted to look like I was in charge. I wanted to demonstrate how hypocritical it is to tell me that . . ." Levi paused. When she spoke again, it was in a perfect Bobbi impression: "When you're in the Miss Liberty costume, you'll behave as Miss Liberty always has. You'll be silent and just dance."

"Bobbi is trying to keep things the same so that people will remember how much they've always loved the parade," I insisted. "We can worry about the voting stuff later. The parade needs our help now!"

"Later?" Levi softly asked. "Savvy, you are so naive. People have to work on democracy every single day. Miss Liberty should remind people that any move that complicates the voting process complicates liberty itself."

Seymour nodded. "Amen!"

"Well, it might be too late for you to defend yourself, honey," Glammy began, patting Levi's hand. "This photo might be the nail in your Miss Liberty coffin."

"But it's a fake photo!"

Levi pinched the bridge of her nose. I knew she was getting a headache.

"Why would someone post a fake picture of you?" I demanded, my voice a little softer this time.

"Maybe now is the time to finally debut my new Miss Liberty costume," Seymour hummed, mostly to himself.

Levi didn't seem to hear him. "Savvy, isn't it obvious? They—whoever *they* are—want to make me look bad."

I stared at her. "Are you actually feeling sorry for yourself?"

"What? No, I—"

"Because you've at least gotten to be Miss Liberty. And Bobbi wanted you to be Miss Liberty again this year to convince everyone to keep the parade here, but you blew it. And look at this flag-burning thing! I don't care if someone photoshopped it, or whatever. People are already freaking out. That means my plans—"

"Oh, Savvy." Levi groaned. "Not your plans again. I'm sick and tired of you always worrying about the future. How we vote today is *the* most important issue."

I slammed my hand on the table and stood up. "The parade *is* the most important issue! Since I was little, I wanted to be Miss Liberty! That's all I've ever wanted, and you're acting like it doesn't mean anything. It's like you chewed up the title and spit it out and it's a piece of gum on the sidewalk and it has no flavor, and I don't care that I'm ranting because it's selfish. *You're selfish!*"

Even as I said it, I knew I was lying. I remembered how I'd felt just a few hours ago as I walked to that voting building. Levi *was* on to something with her voting concerns. But now all I could think about was losing the parade.

"*Excuse me?*" Levi asked, her voice soft but furious.

Glammy raised her hands. "Okay, okay, let's all take a deep—"

"Why can't you just stop hogging the spotlight and go away for five seconds?!" I hollered. "I mean it, Levi. Just go away!"

For a moment, everyone was quiet.

"Savvy . . ." Glammy began, her eyes wide and horrified.

"Whatever!" I cried, pushing away from the table and storming out of the room.

I was face down on my bed when the door opened. The mattress dipped under the weight of someone.

"I believe Levi," Seymour said, "but I also get why you're so mad." He took a deep breath. "I'm going to finish that Miss Liberty costume I'm working on. Just in case."

I kept my face smooshed in my bedspread. "Just in case?"

"Maybe you or Levi will need it."

"Hey, guys!" Dulce's voice floated up the stairs. A second later, she burst into my room and belly flopped onto my bed. "Oh my gosh," she said. "I had to come over! So, this thing with Levi . . . people are losing their minds, which is weird because it's so obvious that the photo is fake."

I rolled over and sat up. "How are you able to tell it's fake? Levi told us, but—"

She held out her phone. "This photo is from the day of our Labor Day barbeque. Remember, Seymour, that was the day you brought all those fake tattoos that your mom had gotten into the shop, and we were putting them on our ankles and arms?"

"Oh yeah," Seymour said. "Your mom freaked when she saw the disco ball on my neck. Thought it was real."

"Exactly." Dulce nodded. "And look, right there, next to Levi, that's an elbow, *my* elbow. You can see it has the butterfly wings from the tattoo I put on. Someone lifted this image and forgot to scrub me out, or whatever it's called, and then they added the image of a burning flag."

"You're right," I said, realizing that she was.

"If you guys are going to have a sleepover, please keep the noise down. I need to crash," Levi said, popping her head into the room.

I stared at her for a moment. She looked younger, like sadness and fatigue were reversing her age.

"Have you been crying?" I asked.

"No. Yes, maybe—"

Just then, a CRASH sounded from the front of the house.

"Now what?" Levi grumbled.

When we got to our living room, I felt the breeze before I saw the rock. Broken glass was on the carpet, on the couch, and strewn across our fake cacti.

Glammy ran to the front door and flung it open. I heard the screech of tires, followed by Glammy's voice. "How dare you! Delinquents!"

Dulce started to giggle. "I'm sorry. It's not funny," she whispered. "I think I'm panicking or something."

I picked up the rock; a piece of paper was wrapped around it. "'Miss Liberty sux,'" I read aloud.

"Nice spelling," Dulce snorted. "It's like when an adult is trying to sound like a kid, only they're trying too hard."

Levi just rolled her eyes and dropped onto the couch. But then she winced, pulling a broken shard from underneath her and setting it on the table.

"I can't believe someone vandalized our home!" Glammy shouted, slamming the door and pulling her phone out of her pocket. "First the trash, then this!"

Levi's arms were crossed over her chest and she had a blank look on her face. I remembered what I said only a little while ago about her being selfish, and I felt sick.

"Are you okay?" I whispered. "When I said selfish, I didn't mean . . . I don't know what I meant. Not that, though."

Levi shook her head "I thought I was just going to talk to people about voting, get them to pay attention. I thought I was doing it in a clever way that was turning heads. But people don't want to hear me. They don't want me to say anything. They want a quiet Miss Liberty, a say-nothing-know-nothing Miss Liberty. They want this last parade to be a sweet and simple show."

This last parade.

Wow. It hadn't sounded real until Miss Liberty herself said it.

"So what did the car look like?" It was the fifth time Officer Catana asked that, but, in his defense, Glammy had changed the color four times.

She tilted her head. "Okay, now that I've had more time, I really do think it was navy blue."

"Not black?" Officer Catana pressed.

"No. Maybe. Well, maybe a blackish blue."

"Any idea about the license plate number?" Officer Sullivan asked.

"There might have been a number three on there."

"Well, we'll check in with the neighbors and see if they saw anything," Officer Catana said, eyeing us like we were his biggest headache ever. "You all have had a busy summer."

"But you know—" Officer Sullivan began. He'd been mostly quiet up until now. "It's understandable that this happened. The photo was insulting. What did your family expect?"

Glammy's face turned bright red, and she crossed her arms over her chest. *"Ex-cuse* me?"

"We'll be in touch," Officer Catana said, looking away from Glammy's glare as he steered his partner out of the room.

When they were gone, Glammy collapsed in the chair.

"Well, that was uncalled for!" She looked at me. "Where is your sister?"

"In her room. Staring up at the ceiling, last I saw."

"We all need to try to get some sleep. The parade is Monday, which means, including today, you all have four days until performance time. Hopefully time is going to fly by and things can get back to normal."

25

I woke up around ten that morning, and Glammy told me that Bobbi had called asking me to head over to the dance studio as soon as possible.

"Did she sound mad?" I asked.

Glammy thought about it, then replied, "Stressed. You want me to go with you?"

I shook my head. I had started this summer wanting to be a professional, and professionals didn't bring their grandmothers along to meetings.

When I arrived, the parking lot was empty except for Bobbi's car. Tiara was standing in the main studio, facing the mirror, slowly lifting her leg in a high developpé. I was mesmerized as she lifted her knee, gradually extending the calf so that her leg made an exquisite line from the floor to the ceiling.

When Tiara saw me in the mirror, she dropped her leg with a thud. "What are you doing here?"

"What are *you* doing here?"

"Bobbi made me come," Tiara said.

"She told me to come, too." I sat under the barres. Then, like we did in preschool ballet, I grabbed the lower bar, lifted my butt off the floor, and started to swing a little.

After a minute of practicing her tendus, Tiara came over and plopped down beside me. She grabbed the barres and started to swing, too.

The office door was thrown open. "I don't care that it's a private business," Bobbi said into the phone. "This is a Fourth of July town. Not a Christmas town. Talk to the Bardots, and I'm sure they'll understand. Or I'll just talk to them myself."

Bobbi hung up the phone. "Is everyone going insane in this town?" she demanded. "Seymour's parents have—get this—turned their store into a *Christmas* shop." She threw her hands up in the air. "No warning. Just a Christmas rebellion in the middle of the summer."

"Mom," Tiara said through gritted teeth. "Who cares?"

"That store sits at the end of the parade route, right by the stage! So any photos of the dancers will have Christmas decor in the background. We need people thinking about summer traditions, not winter ones."

Tiara and I exchanged uncertain looks.

"You know what?" Bobbi clapped her hands. "That's a

battle for later. I'm actually excited. You know, when you finally make a decision that you've been dreading, and then you wonder why you dreaded it in the first place? Well, some serious changes need to be made. Today. Levi is out. And guess who is going to be Miss Liberty now?" She looked between us.

"Me?" Tiara asked in the smallest of small voices.

Bobbi nodded. My heart sank.

"And Savvy!" Bobbi added.

"What?" Tiara and I asked at the same time.

"You are both dedicated, and you both deserve the honor."

"Wait?" Tiara held up a hand. "There are no senior level dancers?"

Bobbi pursed her lips. "Levi was our last one standing. Over the past two years, the others—Kendra, Lori, Deja, Taylor—have all gone on to . . . other things."

It was weird to hear Bobbi say that. I guess Levi took up so much of the spotlight that we hadn't even noticed that she was the last elite dancer of the pack.

"So, that leaves the two of you."

"Mom, people are going to wonder why Levi isn't onstage."

"I don't think they will. With all the fuss she's been causing . . . well . . . we all want a parade that runs smoothly and a show that finishes perfectly."

Bobbi began to pace. "You see—*Levi*"—Bobbi bit on my

sister's name like she was taking a chunk out of a corn on the cob—"for whatever reason, has skewed the optics of the parade by creating a scandal. The only way to snuff out the scandal will be to pop the two of you in and re-create the *wholesomeness* that we're known for. People will see that—they'll feel awash with precious memories, and they'll come to my luncheon the next day and agree that the parade can't go anywhere. I'll get all the signatures I need, go to the Town Council. It's a perfect plan."

For the first time in my life, it occurred to me that saying a plan is perfect doesn't always mean anything. For starters, Bobbi's plan wasn't perfect. People saw the parade last year, and no one rushed to save it when rumors of its ending had started to spread.

"I don't want either of you to worry—you won't be doing the intricate dance number that Levi always does. You'll just be smiling."

"No dancing?" I asked, stunned. "No spotlight?"

"Oh, you'll both have a spotlight. You'll be posing. And every eighth count you can shift into different poses, like this." Bobbi demonstrated with both hands up and flipped, then with one knee bent and the other leg extended. "You two are going to be just like models. Isn't that great? And Dottie is thrilled to be slapping together matching costumes."

I didn't know what to say. I was replacing my sister—not next year, but *this* year. But it wasn't the way I'd imagined.

I was going to be seen, but not dancing. Was that okay? It didn't feel okay.

I studied my reflection, waiting to feel anxious, but the anxiety didn't come. I waited to feel guilty, but guilt didn't come. I had no idea what I felt or what I was supposed to feel.

I suddenly wished someone would tell me.

The second I got home that evening, I told Levi about Bobbi's decision. Secrets had become Tabasco and sriracha mixed together on my tongue. They were spicy and vicious and made my eyes water.

Levi just nodded. She was in bed, her comforter pulled around her. "I know. Bobbi texted me."

"Are you okay? Do you want me to do it, or do you want me to quit, or . . ."

Levi smiled at me, but it didn't quite reach her eyes. "Savvy, I want you to be the best Miss Liberty that you can be. You've been dying for this title, and now it's yours, so have fun."

Then she pulled the covers over her face.

26

The next day, Saturday, July 2, Bobbi was late to rehearsal.

"I'll never forget this date as long as I live," I muttered to myself.

Bobbi was *never* late. Never.

"She's suing my family," Seymour announced to me, arriving a few minutes later. "She's at the courthouse right now, filing paperwork. Mom heard, and she hustled down there too."

"Are you serious?"

Seymour shrugged. "Apparently she's trying to argue that my parents are violating zoning laws or something by changing the store's theme."

Before I could ask what that meant, Bobbi burst into the studio. "All right, performers! On your feet!"

While everyone rehearsed, Tiara and I had to sit in front

of the stage and stretch, watching everyone dance. Because we were watching, we got to witness Bobbi become a very un-Bobbi-like version of herself.

Un-Bobbi-like thing #1: She sat in a chair in the front. Usually she paces.

Un-Bobbi-like thing #2: Instead of showering Miss Libertys with attention, all she said to us was, "Your costumes will be ready soon!"

Un-Bobbi-like thing #3: She was super chipper, as if there was nothing amiss.

"She's using her party hostess smile," Tiara commented with a frown. "That's not a good sign. Whenever she has that smile, it's like she's a robot or something."

"It feels weird to just be sitting here," I muttered.

"Tell me about it." Tiara pulled her legs into her chest. "I asked Bobbi if there was something we could do besides smiling and waving, but she said no. She wants everything to go 'just so.'"

"I could always do a tap solo," I said softly.

Tiara gave me a chiding look. "You are *way* too obsessed with tapping."

"It's the only dance I'm *really* good at."

"That's not true. You're great at ballet."

"Really?" Was my cousin complimenting me?

Tiara sniffed and looked away, like she didn't want the moment to be a "moment." "So . . . how's your sister taking everything?"

"Like you care."

"I actually do. I'm not a horrible person. I'm competitive. I'm a lot like Levi, if you think about it."

I wasn't sure how to take that, so I said, "She's not great. She stays in her room. Glammy keeps making her comfort food." I waited for Tiara to say something. When she didn't, I kept going. "That picture of her is fake, you know. It doesn't even make sense for her to burn a flag. She's trying to draw attention to the fact that the voting location has been moved outside of town."

"Then she should have come out and said it. Honestly, all this costume switching is really immature."

I snorted. "What do you know about maturity? You ditched me that night at Town Hall!"

I was glad to see her flinch. "That . . . was different."

"How?"

"I . . . I . . . got spooked."

"And ran away."

"Fine. And ran away."

She was silent for a minute. "I'm sorry," she finally whispered. "I really feel bad that we bailed on you."

"No you don't."

"Yes I do!"

She kept glancing at me, as if to see whether my

expression was changing. "I can't believe you think I'm lying," she finally muttered.

"Sucks, doesn't it?"

I was surprised when, at the end of rehearsal, Stevie pulled me aside.

"I . . ." She paused and looked over her shoulder, then pulled me toward the corner.

"My mom and I were in Bobbi's office the other day, and Yvette's producer called."

"Yvette Rayne?"

Stevie nodded. "Bobbi had the phone on speaker because she was doing a bunch of other stuff, and the person asked if there were any dancers who might be interested in introducing the weekend weather after Yvette does the five-day forecast at the parade. Just read the weather on the screen or something."

I sucked in a tunnel of air. "Did my aunt—"

"Bobbi said no, there was no one."

And just like that, an invisible hand squished my head like a rotten lemon with Bert inside. "She said no?"

Stevie actually looked bummed. "Maybe your aunt doesn't know you're Little Miss Weather Girl. I mean, your families aren't as close as they used to be, right?"

"Why are you telling me this?"

Stevie looked at her feet. "The trash on your lawn was awful. If that had been my house, I would have died."

I stared at her. Stevie was the nicest of the Tiara & Co. group. No way could she . . .

"And I overheard you saying something about the picture of Levi and the burning flag being fake. It's not right, everything that's being said."

"Do you know who—"

"Stevie, come on!" Mina called from the front door.

"Coming," Stevie shouted. She whispered, "Whoever was on the phone—I think his name was Jett. I remember because he said it was spelled with two *t*'s. Anyway, Jett said if Bobbi knew anyone, just submit a reel or a clip of that person pretending to do the weather forecast."

"Stev-ie!"

"I'm coming, Mina!" Stevie snapped. She looked at me. "Bye."

My head no longer hurt. Maybe I wasn't Miss Liberty, but I could still be proactive.

27

On Sunday, July 3, we had an evening rehearsal, which meant we had the entire day free.

Dulce and I started our morning early in front of Lady Liberty, filming my weather segment. Or trying to.

"So," Dulce said while I figured out how I wanted to stand. "Our slideshow is basically done. All the photos you picked and arranged are in the order you wanted, but I still need a closing slide, just a few words that sum up what we made."

"Okay."

"You don't sound too excited."

I shrugged. "I still want everyone to see it when we're all together. Like at a concert or something."

"Good luck with that," Dulce snorted. "Okay, try not to squint while I'm filming you."

I did my best to widen my eyes.

"Oh, Savvy. No. Now you look like you're doing a zombie impression." Dulce groaned. "Can you just relax your face?"

"I'm trying," I muttered, rubbing my cheeks while looking at my feet. Behind me were 11-by-8-inch poster boards that I had spent all night turning into weatherboards. They were covered with suns, clouds, or rain. A few of the suns had smiley faces, which I now regretted. In my hand was a printout of next weekend's weather. All this was my audition.

"This all might be too late," I said. "The parade is tomorrow, and they called Bobbi over a week ago. Not to mention the fact that today is Sunday and people don't always check email and stuff on Sundays and—"

"I got the parasol!" Seymour cried, running up to us and panting.

"Oh, good," Dulce said. "You got my text. Hand it to Savvy so the sun isn't in her eyes."

Seymour handed me a white parasol that looked like a cupcake with lace.

"Here," he said. "You hold this, and I'll hold up the poster boards and you can just focus on giving the weather report. Easy."

Five takes and an hour later, I snapped the parasol shut and handed it back to Seymour.

"I'm going to email this to Jett now," Dulce said, her fingers flying over her phone.

"What's next?" I asked quietly.

"We wait," Dulce said. "So, just be prepared to do tomorrow's weather, but not so prepared that you're devastated if you don't get to."

I nodded slowly. "So, be prepared to not be prepared because I don't totally know what's happening next?"

"Exactly."

Even though a big unknown hung over me, I couldn't wait to tell Levi what we had done. I felt like I was being proactive, only in my own way.

But when I got home around noon, she was still huddled under her comforter. I poked her, but she didn't even lift her head.

"You look like a burrito," I whispered.

When she didn't respond, I decided to do what Mom always did when we were sick. I tucked the blanket even tighter under her shoulders and her butt.

"What are you doing?" she asked.

"Snug as a bug in a rug."

"Why?"

"You're sick."

"I'm not sick. I've lost my momentum. My mojo."

I thought about *Contact*, the girl in yellow. Everyone else had looked glum, partly because their costumes were in browns and grays. I imagined the girl in yellow making a choice to wear yellow even if she hadn't felt like it.

Levi rolled over and stared up at the ceiling. "Mom and Dad are in California at some massive flea market. Maybe I can afford a flight. Spend the summer touring with them. Forget this town. Forget Miss Liberty."

I tried to think of what I would want someone to say to me if I were in Levi's shoes. "You know what you should do?"

"What?"

"Just go to the parade, walk around, and have fun. I bet people will come up to you and ask about voting. You don't need to be wearing the costume to be our Miss Liberty."

"Maybe."

"Savvy! Where are you?" Seymour called from downstairs.

"Levi's room!" I called back.

Levi pulled her covers over her head as Seymour burst in.

"Oh, hey . . . sorry, Levi . . . I didn't . . . know you were sleeping. Savvy, I gotta tell you something."

"Do you guys mind stepping outside?" Levi said, her voice muffled.

The second we stepped into the hall and I closed the door, Seymour grabbed my shoulders and whispered, "The fireworks are *canceled*."

"What? Why?" The Miss Liberty fireworks were always epic—legendary pyrotechnics that made the town smell like sulfur for days.

Seymour pulled out a fan of peacock feathers and started waving it. "Mayor Radnor came into the bodega. First he told my mom that Bobbi is circulating a petition to have the bodega's displays changed back to the Fourth of July. Then he said that the fireworks were canceled because, and I quote, 'of tensions being what they are.' Oh, and we're also going to have *security*."

"Security?" I asked. "You're not serious?"

Seymour nodded. "Bobbi has hired security guys to walk around in bright orange T-shirts or something. They're going to rope off certain areas, like the front of the stage."

"She thinks Levi is going to pull a stunt."

Seymour nodded. "Is she?"

I looked at the closed door to Levi's room. "I don't think she has the energy to do much of anything."

Not long after Seymour left, there was a knock on the front door. Glammy reached it first and let Officer Catana in.

"A neighbor's security camera caught a glimpse of the person who put trash on your lawn," he said.

"What about the rock incident?" Glammy asked.

He shook his head. "Sorry." Then he showed us the footage.

"They're wearing a hoodie!" Glammy snipped.

But there was something familiar about the person, in the way they kept shifting their weight from side to side.

My expression must have revealed my thoughts, because Glammy poked me. "You know who that is?"

I looked at the officer, at Glammy, and then back to the screen. "No. I mean . . . possibly, but, I mean, no I don't. Sorry."

"It was worth a shot," Officer Catana said.

Glammy walked him to the door, but the second he was gone, she pounced on me. "Spill."

"I think it was Mina's mom, Dottie. She shifts her weight like that all the time. But I don't know for sure."

Glammy scowled. "Give me a percentage. Are you sixteen percent sure? Fifty percent? Seventy-five?"

"I guess ninety-five percent. Or ninety-eight."

Glammy went over to a drawer and pulled out a McDonald's burger wrapper.

"Ew. You saved the trash that was dumped on our lawn?"

"Just this one little piece."

"Why?"

Glammy kissed me on the head. "You have your plan and I have mine. Enjoy rehearsal."

Around four in the afternoon, I started doing my makeup for the night's dress rehearsal. Between foundation and mascara, I kept glancing at Levi's closed door. It felt wrong to be getting ready without her.

"Present!" Glammy announced, startling me. She placed a box in front of me, then whipped the lid off in a *ta-dah* fashion. A phone was inside.

"Oh my gosh!" I screeched. "Thank you, thank you,

thank you! But wait. We can't afford this." Even as I said it, my fingers itched to start dialing Dulce's or Seymour's number.

Glammy waved her hand. "You let the adults worry about what we can and cannot afford. I talked to your parents, and with all the running around that you do, a phone makes sense."

I immediately plopped on the floor, setting the phone in front of me.

"What are you doing?" Glammy asked.

"I have an hour until I gotta be at rehearsal. In the meantime, I'm going to read the entire instruction packet from front to back."

"Of course you are."

28

When I arrived at rehearsal just before six, the sky was laced with a film of cirrostratus, a type of cloud cover where cirrus clouds are spread as thin as fleece from an old pillow, letting you see through to the blue. The street wasn't crowded, but there were a few onlookers watching the Liberty Line dancers as they marked their places for the second time in the last week.

There were barricades keeping the onlookers from approaching the stage. On a table in front of the stage, the mayor had set up his projector, which looked no bigger than a shoebox. That surprised me; I thought it would be big and bulky.

Tiara and I stood in the back, center stage, the flags shooting out of the projector and flashing across our bellies, chest, and knees.

"I hope this doesn't look as weird as I think it does," grumbled Tiara, wiggling her fingers as a flag temporarily tattooed her hand.

I didn't answer. I was trying to remember that being onstage was a big deal; I *should* feel happy and proud. Too bad I wasn't very good at listening to myself.

"Come on," Tiara said. "We're not dancing. Let's chill out on the stairs. If Bobbi gripes at us, we'll say we're guarding the dance bags."

I followed her to the staircase that connected the sidewalk to the side of the stage. It was hidden by a half wall that extended onto the main stage, so no one could see the dancers when they lined up. Everyone had used the alcove to store their dance bags, also known as dancer survival kits. They were filled with protein bars, extra tights, clear nail polish to stop tights from running, and a million-trillion bobby pins.

Of course, my survival kit also contained tap shoes.

I took out my phone for the billionth time to look at the finished reel Dulce had shared with me. I wanted to reassure myself that all the pictures were lined up the way I wanted them.

"Hey, what's that?" Tiara asked, craning her neck as she sat on the step above me. "Pictures?"

"They're Miss Liberty photos. Dulce and I made a slideshow."

"Oh." A pause, and then, "Why?"

I decided that telling Tiara about our plans couldn't

hurt. "We're going to put the slideshow on her website and tell everyone to check it out. I thought the memories could help keep the parade here. Sounds stupid now, but . . ."

My voice trailed off as I looked up at Tiara. But I wasn't really looking at her. I was looking at the back of the stage, at the plain backdrop with the projected flags.

Why didn't I see this before? That backdrop is basically a big screen. What if I hooked up *my* phone to the projector?

I jumped to my feet. "I need to . . . use the bathroom."

Tiara scrunched up her face. "Ew. Porta Potties?"

"No way. The Bardots will let me use theirs."

"Dancers!" Bobbi called from the middle of the stage. "We're having some sound issues. I'm going to give you all a fifteen-minute break, but don't go anywhere. Stretch. Get water."

"Just don't tell Mom you entered the enemy's lair," Tiara said. "In fact, give me your number and I'll text you if she comes looking."

I nodded, gave her the number, and darted over to the Bardots' shop. The second I entered, I heard Dulce's voice.

"Savvy! Welcome to the North Pole," she called.

"Wow," I said, looking around. "What a makeover."

"Makes a person almost want eggnog," Dulce agreed. Then she made an *ick* face. "Almost."

"Where's Mrs. Bardot?"

"In the back. Doing inventory. Our internet at home is

on the fritz. I think my mom forgot to pay the bill. So I came here to sponge off the store."

"You know you can always come to our house."

"Thanks. But I wanted to be close by in case you and Seymour needed me."

I wanted to cry. Sometimes I couldn't believe how lucky I got in the friend department. I hugged her tight. "I love ya."

"Back at you, babe," she said, squeezing my waist.

When I pulled away, I said, "Dulce, I've got it. I know how we're going to make our slideshow *big*! What if, instead of *posting* the slideshow on your website—what if we *play* the slideshow? We'll hook up a phone the way the mayor has hooked up his phone and just let it play. That way, everyone will see it all together. Everyone will get the warm fuzzies! I have a phone now; we can use my phone. I'll hook it up after my weather report!"

I was expecting Dulce to say, *Wow! Great idea!* But she just tilted her head. "But you'll have to be sneaky and unplug the mayor's phone and . . . what about your anxiety? What if you freeze? What if you panic?"

"I won't, Dulce. I *won't*."

I could tell she wanted to believe me, but she didn't.

"Do you really think I can't do this?" I asked.

She adjusted the angle of her laptop screen. "I think . . . when the lights are on the stage and you see everyone in the crowd, and your idol, Yvette, is off to the side, and your aunt is glaring . . . I'm worried you'll feel anxious and you'll panic."

She took my hands in her own. "I'm sorry, Savvy. I just don't want you to freeze and be embarrassed, because I know how that will eat you up. Maybe we should just stick with posting the show online. It's safer that way. No pressure."

I knew what I should say. I should *promise* that my anxiety wouldn't get in my way. I should swear on my tap shoes that nothing was going to make me freeze. But that's not how anxiety worked. It never did what you wanted it to do.

Anxiety was sneaky that way.

So all I said was, "I'm going to do whatever it takes to get my phone plugged in and start our slideshow. I'm going to do my best, I swear. Even if I feel a panic attack coming, or—"

My phone buzzed.

Tiara: *Hurry. Mom is freaking out.* It was followed by an emoji of a head exploding.

I knew I needed to get back, but Dulce's worries about my anxiety bothered me more than I wanted to admit. I was rarely nervous before a show or a recital; I always figured it was because rehearsals made Bert chill.

"That's it! *Rehearsals*!" I cried. "You, me, and Seymour should meet back here tonight. At the stage. Around eleven. Then I can rehearse how I'll get from the stage to the projector to plug in my phone."

Dulce took a deep breath. "Okay. Let's do it. You tell Seymour. We'll all meet here later tonight."

She still sounded skeptical, but I knew she was trying

to have faith in me, and that's really all a dancer with an anxiety hamster in her head can ask for.

When we got back to the stage, Bobbi was standing off to the side, talking to a man I didn't recognize. Tiara waved at me to go join them. As I approached, I saw that the man was wearing a shirt that said Channel 4.

"Are you Savvy?" he asked, extending a hand. "I'm Jett."

"Hi. Nice to meet you."

He tilted his head and grinned. "Listen, I'm a producer who works with Yvette on the weather. We got your video clip and I watched it on the way here—"

"Which I did not know about," Bobbi interjected.

Jett ignored her in a way I had never seen anyone do. "And we'd like to touch base with you about tomorrow's parade. As you are probably aware, we've *never* done something like this before, but we think it will be fun. All you'll have to do is read the temperatures as they are posted on the screen there." He pointed at something that looked like a hanging iPad positioned between the cameras. "You don't have to memorize anything. Just read. Are you okay with that?"

"I don't think this is a good idea," Bobbi said. "Savvy is one of my Miss Libertys. How is she going to deal with the weather and be Miss Liberty?"

Jett frowned. "Oh, really? I didn't realize."

"Quite all right." Bobbi nodded. "But I'm sorry; Miss Rayne will have to do the weather on her own."

"I don't need to be Miss Liberty." I froze the second those words were out of my mouth. *Did I mean that?*

Holy hairspray and hairdos, I did. When I said it, something inside of me relaxed. That uncertain feeling evaporated, and I was filled with a sense of calm.

"What?" Bobbi whispered.

Jett frowned. "Are you sure? I mean, I don't want you to miss out—"

"I have to do the weather." I waved Tiara over. "Are you okay being Miss Liberty by yourself?"

She looked to her mom, to Jett, and then back to me. "Are you sure?"

"I think . . . yes. I'm sure." I couldn't believe what I was saying, but there it was.

"Well, *I'm* not sure!" Bobbi snipped. She looked at Jett. "Savvy . . . well . . . suffers from anxiety—"

"Mom, *stop*. Jeez!" Tiara said.

Bobbi ignored her. "I don't think relying on her when the cameras are rolling is such a good idea."

I wanted to die. No. I wanted to disappear and pretend that I never existed.

Wait, no. I wanted *Bobbi* to disappear. I wanted her to vanish to some island where she couldn't talk about my "issues" or my "problems," or whatever else people called anxiety.

"That's private," I said to Bobbi, my voice shaking. "You had no right. *No. Right.*"

She looked at me, shocked.

"Oh." Jett glanced at me with a furrowed brow.

"I'm fine," I told him. "I'm actually better than fine. I can do this. Trust me."

"But what will she wear?" Bobbi demanded. "What is Yvette wearing? It hasn't been coordinated. Savvy still represents the Liberty Line dancers and . . . and—"

"She has her white T-shirt and navy shorts, Mom," Tiara offered. "If it was good enough for the car wash and Shuckey's Arcade, it's good enough for this."

Bobbi glowered at Tiara. "Thank you, sweetie, but let's get back to poor Savvy's anxiety. I mean, some would say it's crippling—"

"I DON'T HAVE SEVERE ANXIETY!"

If no one was going to listen to my normal voice, shouting was my only option. I glanced at the Liberty Line dancers and at the crowd of people who had gathered by the barricade; then I took a deep breath and turned to Jett. "I don't have anxiety, at least not like my aunt is saying. I'm fine in front of cameras and I'm fine onstage. It's when life is normal that I'm less than fine."

Jett actually chuckled. "So you perform best under pressure? That's what I like to hear."

Bobbi rolled her eyes.

"Okay." Jett clapped. "Sounds like we're back in business. Like I said, you'll just be doing the weekend forecast after Yvette gives the five-day."

Bobbi's eyes were closed, and she was tapping her pearls one by one. She took a deep breath. "Fine. Tiara, you are Miss Liberty, and you are going to remind everyone that she is a gorgeous incarnation of all things patriotic and wonderful, and you're going to make us all feel sparkly and grateful that we live here in the wonderful U.S. of A. Savvy, you'll wear the shorts and shirt from the car wash. But remember, it's still a costume. I want you to treat it as such. Wear some kind of cover-up while you walk around the carnival during the day."

Jett nodded. "Yeah. That sounds like . . . whatever. Great. Savvy, just be as excited as you were in the reel you sent us, and everything will be fine."

Jett shook Bobbi's hand, smiled at me, and walked back to his news van.

Bobbi returned to the dancers. "Let's take it from the top! Tiara, get in your spot. I need to see how it all looks with only one dancer."

"I won't let you down," I called, but Bobbi didn't hear me.

29

I felt a sense of déjà vu as I crept out of the house later that night, leaving behind one snoring Glammy and one snoring Levi. The weather was a balmy seventy-one degrees; the waxing moon glowed blue behind clouds that frothed like cream soda bubbles.

Once I arrived at the stage, I saw Dulce and Seymour.

"This is so cool," Seymour whispered. "Sneaking out. Being here when no one else is around." He handed me the gold and copper costume he had been working on, still protected by the garment bag. "I got your text. Here she is."

"Thanks," I said, laying it on the table where the projector would be. "I want to show it to Levi; maybe it will inspire her to get out of bed. Now, let's do a walk-through of what I need to do tomorrow. The mayor is going to be standing right here." I motioned to the table. "I'll tell him that I have to plug in my phone because the Liberty Line put together a surprise for Bobbi."

"Too risky," Dulce said. "He might stop you. What if I get here early so I can be close to the barricades, and then, when you're ready, I'll wave the mayor over and pretend I have a really important question. That's when you can plug your phone in. Just make sure the slideshow is queued up and ready."

"Perfect," I said, rubbing my hands together. "Let me walk through it."

I went over to the side of the stage where I was going to be standing with Yvette, pretended to signal to Dulce with a big nod, and walked to the projector table in five big steps.

"That was easy," I said.

Feeling that everything was starting to work out, I looked at the sky. The moon had come out from behind the clouds, and I lifted my hands, as if I could hold it like a Magic 8 Ball that would give me answers if I shook it hard enough.

Will the parade go perfectly? Will our surprise work? Will we still have a parade next year? Will I ever be Miss Liberty?

Bert scratched at my brain. I realized that my questions were waking him up, so I tried to shut them down.

"I guess that's it. We're all set," Dulce said, looking around.

"If you feel nervous or whatever, just look for me," Seymour told me. "I'll send my confidence vibes in your direction."

"Cool. Gotcha."

For a minute we all just stood there staring at the empty stage.

"It looks so big and inviting . . . and empty," Seymour whispered.

"It's kind of ours, for tonight anyway," I added.

I realized that there was something I wanted to do, almost *needed* to do. Hurrying over to the side steps, I clambered up to the stage.

"What are you doing?" Dulce called, looking around as if an adult would swoop in at any moment.

"I bet I can get across this stage in five split jumps."

Seymour grinned. "I bet I can do it in four."

I took a running start and began leaping in high splits. But I had too much momentum, and I almost threw myself down the side steps. Stopping short, I landed in a squat, rolled to my knees, and came up laughing.

"How many was that?"

"Five and a half," Dulce called. "Go, Seymour."

Seymour took a hop step and then a baby run before he did four leaps and reached the other side.

"No autographs, please," he announced to an invisible crowd.

"How do you guys get so high off the ground?" Dulce asked, coming up the steps to join us.

"Easy," Seymour said, looking at me. At the same time, we both cried, "Muscles!"

"I have muscles," Dulce said, bending her knees and trying to jump in a split without running.

Seymour walked over and held her by the waist. "Take two little runs, kick your right leg straight in front of you, and jump, pushing off your back leg."

Dulce did as she was told. As she swept her front leg up, Seymour lifted her at the waist to help her get higher. They did three in a row.

"That was fun!" Dulce declared just as the clock at the courthouse chimed, tolling the hour. One in the morning.

"It's really late, you guys," Dulce observed.

"Who cares?" I said. "It's summer."

"Who *cares*?" Dulce asked, looking me up and down. "Did our anxiety-filled Savvy just say 'who cares'?"

Seymour teasingly put a hand to my forehead. "I don't think she's feverish."

"I'm not. I'm . . . excited. Just watch this." I backed up and began to tap, starting with a few traveling shuffles across the stage, swishing my arms back and forth.

Seymour mimicked the steps, and Dulce tried to do the same. I threw in a few riffs, slaps, and cramp rolls. Before long, we were sweaty and ridiculous and happy. I knew we could get into trouble if someone caught us goofing around on the stage, but I didn't care.

Tomorrow I would care. But at this moment, I only

cared that it was summer, I was with my friends, and all my worries were unexpectedly bleached away by a moon that was just as good as any stage light.

We called it a night around two, feeling like the only people in the world. We texted each other to make sure we all got home safe, and then I crashed.

A weather alert woke me at 4:30 a.m. The second I heard the beeping, I panicked. An alert meant a storm or a hurricane or . . . or . . .

It was just an air quality alert for pollen.

I knew I wouldn't be able to fall asleep again, so I got up and took a shower, then put on a leotard and tan tights. Back in my room, my eyes fell on the garment bag that contained Seymour's golden costume. I'd never had a chance to show it to Levi, let alone talk to her about it. It was a costume that deserved to be seen.

Lots of things today deserved to be seen: my sister, the slideshow, the dancers . . . and me.

Without another thought, I unzipped the garment bag and put the costume on, tucking the skirt into my old gym shorts and using one of my dad's button-up shirts to cover the rest of me. It had a pocket in the front, where I put my cell phone.

Once I was covered up, I curled, teased, and hair sprayed my ponytail until it was as perfect as I could make it.

This time tomorrow, the slideshow will have *either* been

a success or not. My anxiety will *either ruin the moment or not.*

I watched the slideshow again on my phone, but something was missing. In the world of dance, there are always opening numbers and concluding numbers.

This needed a conclusion.

What if *I* wrote a conclusion and Dulce edited it? That could work.

Closing my eyes, I remembered the words and images on my sister's wall. Then I started typing in the Chatbox on my phone.

I hit send, then followed up with, *thought you could use some of this for the conclusion.*

That's how Glammy found me when she popped her head in.

"Morning, sweets. You get to meet your idol today. Are we stoked?"

I nodded. "Do you think Levi is coming?"

Glammy pursed her lips "I don't know. I'll see if I can get her out of bed. But . . . you're the first person from the Liberty Line dancers to do the weather. That's a big deal!"

She wasn't wrong. It *was* a big deal. But what if . . . *no, no, no, no. Don't even think about what ifs.*

Glammy kissed me on my head. "I'll see you later today, hopefully *with* your sister in tow. You're doing the weather at seven thirty and the show starts at eight, right?"

I nodded. However, thinking about the day ahead, I had

to ask something. "Um, Glammy, why did you keep that McDonald's wrapper?"

She sniffed. "I'm going to march up to Mina's mom, put it in her hand, and tell her—"

"Please don't."

"Why not?"

"Because, that will start a whole new thread of nasty gossip, and it will hurt Mina's feelings. We know it was her mom and not her. And if she does something again, then we can say something. But for now, just let it go."

Glammy threw her hands up in the air. "Fine. Since I suppose that's mature of you, I'll do as you ask. But if I find out who threw the rock, they're paying for the window."

"Agreed."

"Oh—and Savvy. Your hair looks a little blue. Oh wait, no. It's just the way the bathroom light is hitting all that hairspray. Remind me to replace the bulbs in here. They're quite glary."

I leaned toward the mirror and examined my scalp. There it was, the indigo bursting through the brown, highlighted with sapphire glitter, like streaks on the world's most exotic tiger. Good. I was feeling tigerish.

I met Dulce and Seymour at the carnival.

"Okay, are we ready?" Dulce asked. Before I could answer, she held me by the shoulders. "Now remember, Savvy. You're going to hook your phone up to the cord that's already attached to the projector and hit play. That's all you have to do."

"Got it."

As we walked around the fair, I couldn't help but feel a little disappointed. Usually on the Fourth of July the center of town was like a cauldron bubbling over with people. Last year, I couldn't walk from the Ferris wheel to the bumper cars without tripping over people. The line for the egg scrambler had stretched all the way to Seymour's parents' shop.

Not today. There wasn't even a mini Ferris wheel or an egg scrambler.

Around four, Dulce bowed out. "I need to write," she said. "I'm getting so many *History Fits* ideas, but I'll see you guys soon at the barricade."

It wasn't long after she left us that the evening started to settle in sweet and soft, the sky turning a denim blue as the stars came out one by one.

"It's seven on the dot!" A voice boomed over the speakers. "That means we've got one hour until Miss Liberty and the Liberty Line dancers hit the stage!"

"I gotta meet up with the other dancers for backstage warm-ups," Seymour said. He looked at me. "You good?"

I nodded. "Go do your thing. I'm ready to meet my idol. *Of course* I'm good!"

For about fifteen minutes I stood by myself, looking at the sky. Time seemed to speed up. The sunset no longer eased away; it melted until it felt like it was just me and the cosmos.

The calm was ruined, however, when a woman next to me began speaking.

I recognized her almost at once. It was the Pink Highlighter lady from the grocery store. Next to her was Orange Highlighter. I wondered if they went everywhere in pairs.

"Thank God Levi Montrose was pulled from this show."

"I know! The tux? What does that even have to do with voting? Or Miss Liberty?"

"Maybe she's having a nervous breakdown. You know her parents are trying to open a business. They've been gone for *weeks*."

"Actually—" I jumped in. "Levi Montrose was trying to get everyone's attention so that they'd listen to her about voting."

Orange Highlighter looked me up and down. "Well, the more she talks, the more obvious it is that she's no longer Miss Liberty material." She grabbed Pink Highlighter's hand and stormed away.

"Actually, the more she talks, the more obvious it is that she *is* Miss Liberty material!" I shouted after them.

Next to me, someone laughed. "You tell 'em!"

I whipped around because I knew that voice. It was Yvette. Queen of the Skies Yvette. Stormtracker Yvette. Weather Words Galore Yvette. She was wearing a dress in her signature color, the yellow of marigolds and pineapples, with her dark braids arranged in a crown atop her head.

"Ohmygosh. I watch you every day," I gushed. "And I love everything about you. Your forecasts and your clothes and your hair and your weather words. I'm—I'm doing the forecast with you today."

"Ah! So you're Savvy. Fantastic to meet you." She glanced at her watch. "All right. It's just after seven thirty, and the whole shebang starts at eight. We should head over to the stage. I just *had* to get a soda. I always crave sugar before I go on the air." She held up her cup and shook the ice. "Ready to hustle?"

I nodded. Of course I was!

As we headed toward the side stage, strobe lights suddenly started swooping across the main stage. It felt like the sky immediately darkened, and a white wall glowed just before the flags started being projected across its length.

"Happy Fourth of July!" the mayor bellowed. He was standing in front of the stage, wearing a button-up shirt made to look like an American flag and a bucket hat with flags sticking out of the brim. "Let's give a warm welcome to our Liberty Line dancers!"

The Liberty Line dancers strutted on the stage, and, for a moment, I desperately wanted to be strutting with them. Even Tiara in her Miss Liberty costume strutted onstage before she hit a pose in the back.

I'm supposed to be up there, I thought. *I'm supposed to be part of that group.*

But then I followed Yvette to the side stage and saw Dulce pressed against the barricades, just waiting for me to make my move, and I told myself I was exactly where I was supposed to be.

30

The Liberty Line dancers and Tiara hit their final pose and bowed. The applause was so loud that I swear I could feel it in my molars and cheekbones. For a second, I wished that some of that applause was for me.

Holy hairspray and hairdos, am I jealous?

Even though I was standing with my idol, I was still on the sidelines, missing out on everything that goes with dancing before a crowd. For years, I had wanted to know what it felt like to be up on that stage. I wanted people to say, *Hey, Savvy, saw you on the Fourth of July. You looked good!*

What really stung was that I *could* have been standing there, right next to Tiara, absorbing the applause.

Mayor Radnor stepped onstage. "Hello, Liberté. What

a happy Fourth of July we're having! And how do you like our flag backdrop this evening? Puts us all in the mood, right?"

As Yvette and I waited on the dark side stage, I looked into the audience. I was a little disappointed when I saw Glammy, but no Levi. But then I noticed what Glammy was wearing: a tux! She met my gaze and blew me a kiss.

"*Psst.* Savvy. Are you ready?" Jett whispered, causing me to jump. The last time I had seen him had been when I'd first arrived. He had been off to the side of the stage, talking to important-looking people with headsets. But now his focus was totally on me. "All you're going to do is read what's written on the screen. That's it. You got your costume on under there?"

I nodded, taking my phone out of my front pocket so I could hold it behind my back until it was time. That's when I realized my hands were shaking.

Oh my gosh, I'm really going to do this! Wait—what if it doesn't work. No, no, no. NO anxiety today. Just take this one step at a time. First, you're going to do the weather, then you're going to show off Seymour's costume, then . . .

A spotlight hit Yvette like a bull's-eye, thankfully leaving me in the dark. "All right, Liberté! Thanks so much for having Channel 4 here live! I'm one of your weather hosts, Yvette Rayne."

Yvette stepped a little to her left, revealing the weather screen. The stage where the Liberty Line dancers had performed was now empty, except for the projected flags.

I barely heard her give the forecast. She said something about humidity and barometric pressure. Then, finally, "And those days of pure sunshine will take us all the way to next Friday. But it looks like we might have some stormy skies over the weekend. To talk about that, please welcome one of Liberty's own, meteorologist Savvy Montrose!"

As the spotlight widened to include me, I kept my hands behind my back and looked at the screen. There was the forecast for Saturday and Sunday. All I had to do was read it.

"Well, Yvette, um . . ."

Taking a deep breath, I yanked off my dad's shirt, popping buttons as I did so. In two steps, I kicked off my shorts. A few people in the audience gasped.

There I was, in a costume as gold as those statues they give out at the Oscars.

I would have given anything to see Seymour's face in that moment. I bet his eyes were as big as spotlights. I took a moment to take in the audience; Glammy was giving me a big thumbs-up, and Dulce was near the front, where the guardrails were, her mouth dropped open.

"Oh my storm clouds, Savvy!" Yvette said. "That's quite a costume. I'm feeling underdressed."

"Thanks, Yvette." Light flickered across the gold fabric as I rolled my shoulders back. "So, 'Saturday and Sunday will be seventy-six degrees, with an evening thunderstorm in the mix for Sunday night.'"

"Isn't she a natural, folks?" Yvette asked, and her question was met with applause.

As the clapping died down, I cleared my throat. "Um, actually, Yvette, I'm not quite done. I'd like to say something else, if you don't mind."

I looked at the steps that I'd need to walk down to get to the projector. They suddenly seemed miles away.

"Go on," Yvette whispered, smiling at me.

"Okay, so, um . . . there has been a lot of controversy in town because some people think that Levi Montrose, our Miss Liberty, isn't supposed to talk—but what if something is going on that needs to be talked about? Like vot—"

Out of nowhere, a screech ripped through the air like metal nails scratching an aluminum chalkboard. Then everything went dark.

The audience began to murmur. I didn't move. I was scared that if I did, I'd fall off the stage.

"Hold tight, Savvy," Yvette whispered. I saw the glow from her phone as she whipped it out. "This happened to me once when I was covering a hurricane in Louisiana. Backup generators should start kicking in."

Even though there was no hurricane, it stayed dark. My eyes relaxed as I realized that it wasn't a complete blackout, thanks to the moon. Tonight it was mostly full, a sugar cookie with a bite taken out of it.

"Just a moment, everyone!" Bobbi yelled, but I doubted anyone heard her. Her microphone wasn't working.

"Citizens, stay calm!" Mayor Radnor bellowed next. The moon gave enough light for me to see him unplug his phone and start scrolling. All over the street, squares of light created a glowing checkerboard as people began holding up their phones one after another.

I realized that I could sneak down to the projector, plug in my phone, and be ready for when the power came back on.

But what if the power never comes back on? Will the parade just end like this?

To my right, Yvette and Jett were looking at Jett's iPad and whispering.

"Just give us a few more minutes!" the mayor called.

But no one listened. Instead, people began to jostle one another as they headed away from the stage and back to their cars.

No, no, NO! I had to stop them from leaving. I hurried to the side steps and found my dance bag.

"What are you doing?" Tiara hissed, appearing at my side as I dug out my tap shoes.

"I'm going to get people to stay."

"*What?* What are you—there's no electricity, Savvy!"

"There's the moon."

I was on a mission. As I clickety-clacked onto the stage, I could feel the moon's rays on me, and I knew people could see me.

My taps started soft, then became louder. On and on I went, just winging it, the rhythm in my brain taking over. It was easy in the dark; I could be fearless in the dark.

I performed a sequence of taps that we always did during warm-ups. Nothing fancy, but it always sounded cool, and it got us revved up for class. It consisted of three separate sixteen-count combinations of shuffles, taps, heel drops, cramp rolls, and riffs. I just kept repeating them over and over.

Someone fell into step to my right. It was Tiara. A moment later, another dancer started repeating the steps on my left: Seymour.

I heard more dancers joining behind me. Together, we repeated the steps, and the sound exploded like a rainstorm as three dancers became four and then four became six and six became nine. When I added a half-turn, I saw that every Liberty Line dancer was behind me.

The crowds started clapping.

"Go, Savvy!"

"Whoo-oo! Go Liberty Line!"

At those magic words, my heart swelled, and then the lights came back on, flooding the stage, almost blinding us. But we were moving in such perfect unison that it was easy to keep on dancing.

Letting my arms swing with the rhythm, I spied my sister, wearing a red tank top, right in the middle of the crowd. Even from the stage I could see that she had a stack of papers in her hands and was passing them out.

I did a sequence so that my back was to the audience and I could face my fellow dancers. As we tapped out another eight count, I brought my arms up like an orchestra conductor telling my musicians it was time to slow down, and then I dropped my hands.

"*And stop!*" I mouthed.

As if we had been practicing for ages, we all finished on a *bud-a-bump-ba*.

Applause, applause, and more applause, the kind I had been craving all summer.

"Wait! One more thing!" I shouted to the audience.

I jumped off the front of the stage, feeling like a rock star.

Dulce saw me and started waving her arms at the mayor. "Mayor Radnor! Can I get a quote from you about what just happened with the electricity?"

He hesitated. "I'm kinda in the middle—"

"That's fine," Dulce said offhandedly. "I suppose I could make something up about tonight's power outage. Maybe our grid was overwhelmed? Maybe local government didn't fund it properly?"

The mayor hurried over to her. "You know what, I can spare a minute."

I pulled up the slideshow and plugged in my phone. For a second, I didn't dare turn around. Then I saw that people in the audience were staring, so I looked, too.

"It worked." I sagged with relief. The first image was of Bobbi and Levi. I remembered thinking I had to start with that one. Over the image were the words *Miss Liberty's Greatest Hits: A tribute brought to you by Savvy Sienna Montrose and Dulce Marie Montoya.*

"Everyone!" I called at the top of my lungs. "Please enjoy this homage to the Miss Liberty Independence Day Parade, a show that belongs to our town, and our town alone!"

The next picture was of the Liberty Line dancers rehearsing, followed by photos of unknown dancers chilling out on the sidelines and stretching. There was a picture of Mina's mom at the sewing machine, and one of a 1967 Miss Liberty posed on a surfboard onstage under a sign that said *Hello summer.* Then the reel went back to 1951, when the town held a Thanksgiving Day Parade and Miss Liberty had her own float. That was followed by images of Levi when she was Miss Liberty for the very first time and her shoes had been spray-painted with red glitter.

That was the year I began using the phrase Glitter Season to describe these summer days. Funny, I had forgotten this until now.

"I think this is the part where you say more," Yvette whispered.

I jumped. I hadn't noticed that Yvette had come to stand beside me.

"I didn't—I didn't prepare anything," I whispered back.

"Who said anything about preparing? Just talk."

I hesitated.

Yvette bent so that she was eye level with me. "Clearly,

this parade means a lot to you. No shame in sharing that passion." She handed me her microphone.

I looked at the backdrop, at the photos of laughing and crying Miss Libertys, Liberty Line dancers wearing go-go boots, and Liberty Line dancers wearing heels with bows on their toes. There were Liberty Line dancers with teased bangs and Liberty Line dancers with hair straight and sleek. They made it seem as though Miss Liberty had been around since the beginning of time.

I walked back onstage, keeping to stage left so my head wouldn't block the images. Licking my lips, I realized that I was perfectly calm, and in that calm, I *did* have something to say.

"I bet you all have photos of the parade at home, that they make you remember that Miss Liberty isn't just important because she's a symbol of American pride and freedom, but because she's *our symbol*. She's here to remind us what is important to our town. She's something we can look forward to, even when we're stressed-out or worried. Miss Liberty is always there, promising at least one day and one night of fun.

"But Miss Liberty is bigger than fun. My sister said something about how fighting for democracy needs to be part of our everyday lives. I didn't understand that at first, but I'm starting to get it now."

On the screen, Miss Liberty of 1977 posed with the high school marching band in front of the old Liberté fairgrounds. Then Miss Liberty 1992 was standing in front of a *Rock the Vote* poster.

"Each of these Miss Libertys reflected a fight for freedom that was happening in her time. It could have been about lowering the voting age, or men and women getting paid the same. Maybe they didn't say it out loud, like our current Miss Liberty has been, but the connection was always there. I think people haven't cared much about losing the Miss Liberty parade—we've gotten too comfortable thinking liberty will always be right here. But the voting center is forty-five miles outside of town, and that means it's inconvenient to get to. We can't let our freedoms be inconvenient. They should be . . . well . . . convenient."

I caught my sister's eye. I was pretty sure she was smiling.

A slide popped up with just one image: the Liberty Lady statue. Next to her were words. *My* words.

THIS SLIDESHOW IS IN HONOR OF ALL LIBERTY LADIES WHO HAVE STOOD TALL AND CONFIDENT. IT IS ALSO FOR THOSE LIBERTY LADIES WHO ARE JUST BEGINNING TO LEARN HOW TO STAND TALL AND CONFIDENT. AND IT'S FOR THE LIBERTY LADIES WHO BELIEVE IN THEMSELVES AND IN WHAT'S RIGHT, WHO ARE SPARKLY AND FIERCE, AND WHO KNOW THAT THE TIME TO BE SILENT IS NEVER.

The slideshow ended. I felt like there wasn't much else to say, except "Thanks for your time."

I hit the toe of one tap shoe behind me and curtsied more gracefully than I had ever curtsied before.

31

THE DAY AFTER:
FROM THE DESK OF DULCE MARIE MONTOYA

Change doesn't happen in a day; it takes stamina and patience. Let's talk about voting. In school, we're taught that after the Nineteenth Amendment was passed in 1919 and ratified in 1920, women had the right to vote. But did they? In reality, white women were given the right to vote, but nonwhite women were blocked from voting because of poll taxes, literacy tests, and many other barriers and forms of violence and intimidation. Native American women got the right to vote in 1924 and Chinese American women in 1943. It wasn't until 1965 that President Johnson signed the Voting Rights Act into law, which fought against voter discrimination.

However, voting discrimination still exists, in the form of gerrymandering and limited locations. That is what our current Miss Liberty wants us to remember and fight against. And when she's talking, shouldn't we listen?

When I left the house around eleven the next morning, I wasn't sure where to go. On one side of town, Levi was hosting a protest to get support; on the other, Bobbi was hosting a luncheon to get signatures.

And I was standing in the middle of it all, on the corner of Constitution Avenue and Amendment Way.

When I woke up that morning, part of me thought that I was a different person, an assertive person, cured of my anxiety. But then I felt Bert yawning, and I knew that anxiety would probably always be a part of me. Luckily, I was learning to roll with it.

Last night I had thought that either Levi would give up her protest or Bobbi would give up her luncheon and the two would unite, like in some superhero movie.

But when I talked to Glammy that morning, she said, "Don't hold your breath. You did an excellent job, and I'm so proud of you, but you gotta let others figure things out for themselves."

Now, standing on the corner, I could see a few people walking across the street toward the courthouse. That made me think Levi was doing okay, that people were supporting her. But I was worried about Bobbi. She and I had been in this together; I had to go check on her. I owed it to her.

When I walked into the dance studio, the first thing I saw were tables covered with waffles, fruit, sausage links, bacon, and every flavor of bagel in the universe. Another table had lunch foods: sandwiches, fruit salads, and cold pasta.

"Nothing like a buffet that's a little lunch and a little breakfast, am I right?" Bobbi called. She was sitting on a foldout chair as if it were a throne.

"Well, come on in, Savvy. Eat. Dottie went to get coffee, but there's orange juice in the pitcher and soda in the ice cooler."

"Where is everyone?"

Bobbi's lips pursed into a pale pink line. "The mayor stopped by earlier. As for everyone else, I'm sure that most Liberté residents are sleeping in after yesterday's dynamo performance. Not to mention that you're here, and if anyone was going to take Levi's side, it would be you. Your slideshow was a lovely touch, by the way. Of course, I wish you had warned me—that would have been nice—but I guess you're rebellious, like your sister."

I wasn't sure how to take that, so I just said, "I'm actually desperate to keep the parade here, to keep Miss Liberty here. That's why Dulce and I put the slideshow together. We thought it would help people remember how much they loved it."

"And you did an excellent job; it was a very sentimental touch."

"*But*," I continued, "that's not going to cut it. I think we have to look at Miss Liberty a little differently. She can't stay a silent icon. She's got to be allowed to talk, to have causes and raise awareness."

"Allowed to have *causes*? Savvy, I've been running this parade for a long time. Just because your sister—"

"Do you know what the Fujiwhara Effect is? It's when two hurricanes or storm fronts dance around each other because they have a common center. Eventually they either merge or split off and go in different directions."

"Why are you telling me this?"

"I think you and Levi should merge together or, I guess, go flying off into different directions, into different towns. Of course, that would be sad—Liberté without its two most famous Miss Libertys."

Bobbi twisted two fingers around her pearls. They were the biggest pearls she owned, the jawbreaker pearls.

"Bobbi, come with me. Come to Levi's protest."

I could tell she was seriously thinking about it, and, for a moment, I thought she'd get up, take my hand, and leave with me.

But then she sighed heavily. "Maybe later. But I can't leave just yet. What if someone shows up?"

Later that afternoon, I saw Levi in front of the courthouse. I wasn't sure if anyone was working there, but that didn't stop people from picking up the signs she had apparently been making—signs with such slogans as *We want our voting location back!*

"Hey!" she said. "I was worried that you'd been roped into Bobbi's thing."

"I stopped by. It was kinda sad. No one was there, but she had a lot of breakfast foods out. I asked her to come here, but I don't know if she will."

Levi shook her head. "She won't. Bobbi is a traditionalist."

"What do you mean?"

"You know how you get anxiety when things feel like they're too much? Bobbi feels the same. Only she purses her lips and pulls on her pearls and tries to act cool and together, like her anxiety isn't pulling her in a million different directions. Change makes her more anxious than anything else. And if there's the slightest chance she'll be able to halt the change, she's going to dig her heels in and do it. That's why I've always admired her. She at least is gutsy when she believes in something. I'm just at odds with her right now about what's important. The people who are here are here because they care. If the town is open to Miss Liberty changing into a more proactive mascot, we might just convince Bobbi and keep our parade. We all have to be willing to change to stay relevant."

Throughout the day the crowd in front of the courthouse grew steadily. Around four in the afternoon the Channel 4 van showed up and Yvette popped out, dressed in a sequined red, white, and blue skirt and a white blouse with gold buttons the size of meatballs.

"Hello, Savvy!" she called.

"Hi. I like your outfit. Very thematic."

"After last night, I knew I had to be here. You've got a town fighting to keep its voting location *and* its parade. If that's not a story with local interest, I don't know what is."

Seymour appeared beside me and put an arm around my shoulders. "Savvy is pretty fierce, wouldn't you say?"

I rested my head in the crook of his neck.

"So fierce," Yvette agreed. "So very, very fierce."

That evening, there was a sherbet sunset. As far as I knew, that was not an official weather term, but what else could I call a sky that looked sweetened with pinks and oranges?

As the sun was melting, I got a text from my mom.

Am I your first text?! (She followed that with a heart and a winking emoji.)

Ha ha! Sorry. Dulce has that honor. I added a smiling face.

Dad and I are driving through the night. We'll be seeing you guys tomorrow afternoon. We've got so much to talk about. Good change is on the way!

I sent back six heart emojis and a kiss and waited for Bert to react to the reality of more change, but he remained still.

That surprised me. After all, I was suspended on an in-between planet that was orbiting several possibilities at once. Nothing had been decided for sure. Not for me, or for the town, or for the parade. We all were waiting.

Would the parade stay or go? Would the voting location come back or remain way out in the middle of nowhere?

I had no idea.

I had no plan.

I had no trajectory.

And that was scary. Part of me wished that my weather watch had a fortune-telling app. Then again, even if I had that, I'd probably find a way to worry about something else.

Maybe all I can do is try to remember what Dulce had written about change: It doesn't happen overnight or all at once. It requires stamina and patience, and we should just get out of bed and start making it happen, because really, what else are we going to do?

Even if I do everything I'm supposed to, part of me will always worry, and that's okay. At least I'm starting to figure out how to breathe in between worries, how to just look up at the sky from time to time—guessing the weather, admiring the moons, and naming the sunsets—eventually finding some kind of sweet spot between feeling a little bit anxious and a whole lotta fierce.

ACKNOWLEDGMENTS

This book would not have been possible without the unflinching support, absolute love, and creative craziness of my family:

Mom: No one sees the positives in life like you do, and I am forever grateful for the strength of your optimism. Thank you for always believing in me, especially during my moments of rocky doubt. Perhaps most importantly, thank you for your adventurous spirit and for hopping in the car to take not one but two epic cross-country road trips with me while I chased the writing muse. No one embraces life like you do!

Dad: Thank you for filling my life with art and artistic daredevilry. Watching your dedication only fueled and inspired my own, and the stories in each of your exquisite paintings always fill my head with possibility. Thank you for reading *Scary Stories to Tell in the Dark* at nearly every slumber party I ever had, for taking me to my first Harley-Davidson show, and making props galore for all those recitals.

Jorden: Thank you for being the big brother who always let me tag along, for taking me to my first Tori Amos concert and for introducing me to the storytelling worlds of *The Dark Crystal*, *Vampire Hunter D*, *Usagi Yojimbo* and a million others. Thank you for all the NYC trips and for the creative oasis that is Birdovprey.com.

There is no way that this book would have seen the light of day without my extraordinary agent, Molly O'Neill. You always know what story I am trying to tell and your patience, support, and genius have been invaluable. From inception to execution, you have always been there, and I cannot wait to see where we go next!

Thank you to my fabulous editor, Amy Cloud. I never would have taken this book as far as it has gone without your narrative artistry. You helped me launch Savvy and her friends off the page in a way that I never thought possible. Thank you!

To my Barnes & Noble family at Exton Main Street (#2086), a massive thank you! I loved every minute of working with you all and I know that young minds especially will thrive as long as booksellers like you nurture them with stories and help them challenge themselves through fantastic tales.

Finally, no acknowledgments would be complete

without a shout-out to my writing professors at the University of the Arts in Philadelphia. It devastates me that the school has closed its doors, for it was under your tutelage that I received the training to take writing as far as I could.

To my readers, thank you for coming along on this journey.